"JIM!" McCOY SAID INTO HIS COMMUNICATOR.

"Beam us out of here right now! And get Sulu—he's about a hundred meters away from us."

As Spock awaited rescue, he and the doctor continued to retreat from the green wall, which was now some seven meters high and seemed to be all of an endless piece rising from the crack in the ground. More fissures formed; Spock leaped over a crack as it ran past him.

"This wall," McCoy was saying, "this mass . . . it's what destroyed the town."

"I am well aware of that, Doctor," Spock said, peering at his tricorder.

STAR TREK®

ACROSS THE UNIVERSE

PAMELA SARGENT
AND
GEORGE ZEBROWSKI

POCKET BOOKS
New York   London   Toronto   Sydney   Tokyo   Singapore

An *Original* Publication of POCKET BOOKS

POCKET BOOKS, a division of Simon & Schuster Inc.
1230 Avenue of the Americas, New York, NY 10020

STAR TREK is a Registered Trademark of Paramount Pictures.

A VIACOM COMPANY

This book is published by Pocket Books, a division of Simon & Schuster Inc., under exclusive license from Paramount Pictures.

ISBN: 0-671-01989-9

First Pocket Books printing October 1999

10 9 8 7 6 5 4 3 2 1

POCKET and colophon are registered trademarks of Simon & Schuster Inc.

Printed in the U.S.A.

To Greg—

thanks again

Chapter One

LEANDER CORTÉS had known for some time that he was a dead man, that the vessel carrying him and his shipmates would become their tomb.

Why had he and his companions insisted on clinging to life, even while knowing they were condemned? Perhaps, he thought, in the hope that, if they were ever found by other voyagers across the interstellar ocean, it would be seen that they had fought against death right up to the end. Maybe most of them had gone on breathing and living only out of habit.

He did not know what his shipmates were thinking now. They had not said much to one another for a while, as if preparing themselves for the absolute silence that would soon claim them all.

Cortés floated weightlessly in the forward control room of his ship. The relativistic craft had lost its gravitational effect, simple acceleration against decks, nearly a year ago when the drive failed, but the vessel had been slowing down long before that. He and those with him had accepted the fact that they were not likely to arrive at their destination until they were past the prime of their lives. They had to take only one more small step further to realize finally that they would never reach that world at all.

He had grown so used to the nearness of death, so accustomed to the thought that he was almost ready to welcome his end . . . and then, suddenly, a voice had called out to him across the universe.

The voice was a human voice, a male voice, speaking to him in a language he could understand, a language that had hardly changed in all the years that had passed since he and his comrades had left Earth. Another interstellar voyager had crossed the path of Cortés's ship while searching for him and his shipmates. The man had asked him for permission to come aboard.

Cortés could not remember exactly how he had replied, but by the time the stranger managed to reach the nearest airlock in whatever sort of shuttlecraft he possessed and board the ship, perhaps—

No, Cortés told himself. The chance of anyone—of any other intelligence—actually finding his ship was practically nonexistent. No one from Earth could be searching for him now, and no alien was likely to address him in any language that he knew. There had been no voice from another ship; he had only imagined that a rescuer was coming for him.

Now, suddenly, a bright ghostly shape was forming in front of him. Before he could cry out, a man appeared, and then another, and then three more human figures behind them.

I am going mad, Cortés thought; these apparitions could not be real. He watched in disbelief as they reached out and grabbed at rungs and handholds.

"Captain Cortés." He had heard that voice before, over the ship's radio, the voice of his imagined rescuer; it came from the young light-haired man who was hanging closest to him. "Captain Cortés, I am James T. Kirk, captain of the *U.S.S. Enterprise.*" Another of the apparitions floated toward Cortés, and he was suddenly aware of this being's pale skin and long, pointed ears.

"We come in peace," the illusion called Kirk continued. "You have nothing to fear from my companion with the pointed ears. He's my first officer and science officer, Commander Spock—he is a Vulcan."

Well, that explains everything, Cortés thought wildly, not understanding, fearful that the strangers might not be human after all, and then the darkness he had been waiting for swallowed him.

"Captain Cortés." Another voice was calling to him through the darkness. "Captain Cortés."

He was lying against something that felt like a couch or a bed. Cortés took a breath, then realized that he was no longer floating, that gravity had slipped its bonds over him once more.

He forced his eyes open, blinking against the light. An auburn-haired man with a concerned expression on his face was gazing down at him. This man, Cortés realized, was the twin of one of the apparitions that had so suddenly materialized in the control room of his ship.

"Captain Cortés," the man said again, "I'm Doctor McCoy, chief medical officer of the *Enterprise*. We're beaming the rest of your people aboard as quickly as possible for treatment—we've already filled all the biobeds near yours with new patients."

"What?" Cortés said, trying to grasp what the stranger was saying.

"You'll be all right," the man said. "You had better rest now, start getting your strength back."

Was that even possible? Cortés wondered. He had been ill for so long; would he ever be well again? Then he closed his eyes and let himself sink into unconsciousness again, and dreamed of his deliverance from death.

Chapter Two

JAMES KIRK leaned forward and rested his arms on the table top. Except for Dr. McCoy, all of the officers he had summoned to the briefing room were present. Since Ilsa Soong, one of the other medical officers, was already seated at the table, Kirk decided not to wait for McCoy.

"Dr. Soong," Kirk said, "we'll begin with your report and assessment of our new passengers."

"All of the people from the *Hawking* are resting now," Lieutenant Commander Soong said. "The ones who seem strongest have been assigned to crew quarters, and the rest are sleeping in sickbay. Dr. McCoy will probably have more to say when he gets here, but fortunately all of their physical problems are conditions we can treat."

The physician paused for a moment. Kirk waited, seeing that she had more to tell him.

"Physically, I'm sure all of Cortés's people will recover quickly," Soong continued, "but psychologically it's going to be a long haul for them. They're temporally displaced and at least a few seemed mentally unbalanced. Under the circumstances it's a wonder none of them committed suicide. That's the one thing that gives me a bit more hope for their eventual mental recovery."

Captain Cortés's craft, a relativistic vessel called the *Stephen Hawking,* had left Earth nearly two centuries ago. The Federation ship *Hoyle* had been the first to encounter the old starship, but had kept away, since the *Hoyle*'s crew had no standing orders to make contact in such a situation. After the *Hoyle*'s commanding officer, Commodore Shirley "the Cat" Spencer, told Starfleet of what she had found, a data specialist had discovered that a Federation historian had unearthed information about this particular obsolete ship and its probable position. The *Enterprise,* under Starfleet orders to investigate, had already been on its way to explore the old craft by the time Commodore Spencer had discovered the long-forgotten ship from Earth.

"Another piece of the past, still coming at us," was the way Cat Spencer had put it in her message to Kirk.

"Thank you, Dr. Soong," Kirk said. "Lieutenant Longstreet, I assume you've already begun preparing a historical summary for the people from the *Hawking.*"

Farley Longstreet nodded; the young officer was an information systems specialist as well as a historian with a thorough knowledge of Earth's early and middle twenty-first century. "Filling them in on the history that has passed while they were on their voyage is going to be interesting," Longstreet said. "These people knew they were leaving their own time behind, but they expected to settle another planet without ever knowing what had happened on the world they'd abandoned. Now that future world has reached out to grab them. They're going to find out what has happened. They'll have to deal with a future they never expected to encounter, and somehow adapt to it."

"We can tell them what they escaped," Lieutenant Hikaru Sulu said. Kirk knew what Sulu meant. The *Hawking* had left Earth about fifteen years before World War III.

"True," Longstreet said, "and that's just what worries me. They'll find out that people they knew—people they cared about—probably died during the nuclear winter that followed our last world war."

Lieutenant Uhura glanced at Longstreet. "But they'll also learn that there were survivors," she said, "and that Earth recovered from that war. They'll learn that humankind is finally at peace with itself, if not necessarily with some of the races in this galaxy."

"Permission to speak, Captain," Ensign Pavel Chekov said then. "I have discovered something else about our guests—about one of them, in any case."

Kirk nodded at the ensign. "Go ahead, Mr. Chekov."

"I have learned that one of the men we brought aboard is Dmitri Sergeievich Glakov, an ancestor—a relative from the past—of mine. His name was on the *Hawking*'s manifest. I do not know much about him except that he left Earth in the early years of space travel and—"

Chekov looked down for a moment before continuing. "He was something of a rogue, Captain. According to the family stories I heard, he was involved in some shady ventures. I do not think they could have been great offenses, because by that time the worst criminals among my countrymen had been put away, so to speak, but I thought you should know."

"Very interesting," Kirk said.

"I suspect that when Dmitri Sergeievich Glakov disappeared from Earth," Chekov went on, "he was trying to escape the consequences of some of his illegal acts. For many in my family, he was regarded as a most colorful character—they would tell tales passed down to them about Dmitri Sergeievich shooting it out with rival gangs and riding around Moscow in a stolen limousine, a beautiful woman on each arm."

Commander Spock raised a brow. "Fascinating," the Vulcan officer said.

"I do not know how many of those stories are true." Chekov frowned. "Many of them probably grew in the telling. But I do know that there was much criminal activity in my homeland during that time, and that Dmitri Sergeievich Glakov was not what you would call a respectable citizen. Now he is aboard our ship." He sighed. "At least now I know what happened to him. Of course, I would like to learn more."

"I'm sure all of your relatives will also be interested to find out about him." Kirk looked around at the other officers. "Scotty, I want you and an engineering crew to scan the *Hawking* thoroughly as soon as possible and find out if it's worth salvaging."

Lieutenant Commander Montgomery Scott nodded. "Aye, Captain. And we'll beam aboard to take a look around when we know more about her."

"We also have to find out something about the *Hawking*'s original destination star," Kirk said, "and whether or not there are habitable planets in its system."

Spock turned toward the captain. "I have already put in a search," the science officer said, "to learn if that system has ever been visited."

Kirk leaned back. "We'll have to assemble the *Hawking*'s crew and passengers as soon as possible and find out from them what they wish to do. By then, we should know if their destination star holds a viable choice of habitable planets or not."

Spock raised a brow and said, "The *Hawking*'s people may be most confused about their future plans, given what they have already learned about their situation."

"Granted," Kirk said. "We must hear from them before we decide anything. Once they have a clear idea of their options, we'll do what we can to assist them."

Uhura lifted a hand. "Captain," she said, "I'm sure there must be several colonial settlements that would willingly accept a hundred people. That might be better than giving them a world to win entirely on their own, in isolation."

"I agree, Lieutenant," Ilsa Soong murmured, "but I suggest that we assemble the people from the *Hawking* in groups of twenty for discussion, rather than all of the one hundred in one group."

"Oh?" Kirk said. "And why?"

"My feeling is that being brought together in one large group for a meeting would prevent many from voicing their true feelings," the physician replied. "Larger blocks might affect minority opinions, but in smaller groups those opinions would become available to us, rather than being suppressed."

"Suppressed?" Kirk asked.

"We don't know the dynamics of this community, Captain," Uhura said. "I agree with Dr. Soong. People might remain silent out of fear of rejection, afraid to say what they really think. In smaller groups, they're likely to be more open. These people have been trapped aboard their ship for quite some time. I doubt they could have survived that experience without forming strong bonds and keeping a lot of possibly disruptive feelings to themselves. They may be especially reluctant to speak their minds too freely in a large group."

The door at the end of the briefing room slid open, and Leonard McCoy came inside and sat down quickly at the other end of the table. The chief medical officer looked harried and more than a little annoyed.

"Anything to tell us, Bones?" Kirk asked.

McCoy took a deep breath and said, "Our new passengers are all very run down, and are suffering from calcium loss and muscle atrophy from being gravity-deprived for so long. Several are anemic, several others have sinus and respiratory infections, all of them have malnutrition and damaged immune systems, and a few show signs of injuries from earlier accidents—broken and knitted bones, contusions, and the like—fortunately, none of them serious. We're doing all the physical reconstructive work quite easily, but I can't speak for the state of their minds."

All of the officers were silent for a few moments. Kirk thought of his first encounter with Leander Cortés aboard the *Hawking*. The man had been so gaunt that he had looked like a figure out of an El Greco painting, floating weightlessly with his long gray hair fanning out from his head. The unconscious man Kirk had held while beaming back to the *Enterprise* had been hardly more than a bag of bones in his arms.

At last Kirk said, "I'm certain their spirits will improve with restored health."

"There's no question that improved health will banish some of their mental distress," Ilsa Soong said, "but it will also present them with new problems."

McCoy nodded. "You're right. Some will make it, but there may be others who won't recover emotionally, at least not any time soon."

"Hope can only grow," Kirk said, "from new, positive experiences. We'll just have to make sure these people get those experiences."

McCoy sighed. "Easier said than done, Jim. The greatest unknown is still in the human mind."

Spock lifted a brow. "Not quite, Doctor," Spock said. "The greatest unknowns exist inside intelligent minds."

"Yes, Spock," McCoy said, "and even inside literal-minded Vulcan minds. But the unknowns I'm most concerned about right now are Leander Cortés and his people."

Chapter Three

PAVEL CHEKOV had approached his kinsman cautiously, wanting to make certain that Dmitri Glakov could handle the shock of finding out that he had a descendant aboard. At last he had managed to take Glakov aside for a cup of tea in one of the small meeting rooms near sickbay. After only a few days aboard the *Enterprise,* the older man already looked much improved. There were fewer silver strands and more chestnut ones in Glakov's thick head of hair, and his thin sharp-cheekboned face had begun to fill out.

"It is good to talk with a countryman from my future, Pavel Andreievich," Glakov said in Russian as Chekov handed him a cup of tea. "It is even better to hear my mother tongue spoken by you and to know that it has not changed beyond recognition."

The man's dark eyes were warm, his expression open; he did not strike Chekov as a criminal, although a skilled

confidence man or swindler might seem equally congenial. He had introduced Chekov to a few of his companions, none of whom had seemed especially uneasy
around Glakov. All of that, Chekov reminded himself,
might mean only that his relative had formed strong
friendships aboard the *Hawking,* which was not surpris-
ing given what he and his comrades had faced.

"You will find much new terminology in our language
that is unfamiliar to you," Chekov said.

"I already have." Glakov drank from his cup. "But then
I would have expected that. New words I can learn, Pavel
Andreievich. That will be the least of my problems."

"That is so, Dmitri Sergeievich." Chekov wondered
how to broach the subject of his ancestor's past.

"It is also gratifying to know that Russia, and of course
the rest of Earth, has become the kind of world so many
of our people once hoped for and envisioned. To tell you
the truth, it did not seem such a likely prospect in my
time."

"I know how hard those times were," Chekov said.
"We Russians have a long memory for our suffering. Stories of the past came down to me from my father and my
mother, and from my grandparents." He paused. "But
there is something I must tell you, Dmitri Sergeievich. I
hope it does not come as too great a shock."

Glakov leaned forward and rested his arms on the table
top. "Say what you have to say. I have already survived
many surprises during the past few days."

Chekov cleared his throat. "On my mother's side, my
grandfather had a direct male ancestor by the name of
Mikhail Sergeievich Glakov, who had an older brother

named Dmitri. They were both born in Zagorsk, but their parents moved to Moscow a few months after the birth of their second son. It means—"

"—that you are part of my family," the other man finished, obviously drawing the correct conclusion immediately. "You are a descendant of my brother!" Glakov reached across the table and clasped Chekov's right hand between two palms. "But this is remarkable! Now that I know that, it seems to me that there is indeed something of my brother Misha in your face."

"And I have heard some stories about you," Chekov said, "and about your life in Moscow."

Glakov was still looking at him with anticipation in his eyes. He did not seem like a man afraid that a sordid past might now come back to haunt him. "And what did you hear?"

Chekov took a breath. "One of the more exciting tales was of an armed robbery you committed at a jewelry store on Gorky Street in broad daylight. Another was of a high-speed chase in automobiles to a town almost two hundred kilometers outside Moscow, where you were at last able to make your escape. But I think my favorite is the shoot-out you had with some hoodlums in a Moscow cemetery, as if your gang and its rivals were at the O.K. Corral of the old American West . . ." Chekov's voice trailed off. Perhaps his tone had been a bit too enthusiastic.

Glakov gaped at him. Chekov tensed, keeping his hand near the phaser at his waist. Then Glakov threw back his head and laughed.

"A high-speed chase!" He shook his head and laughed

again. "A shoot-out in a cemetery! Pavel, I am sorry to disillusion you, but my life on Earth was not nearly so eventful as that."

Chekov stared at him, not knowing what to say.

"My sides are aching! I thought I had lost the power to laugh!" Glakov gradually stopped laughing and grew calmer. "I will confess that I was not always on the right side of the law," he continued, "but my illegal activities consisted largely of black-market currency transactions and picking an occasional pocket. As for gangs, the only ones I had contact with were the ones to whom I sometimes had to pay protection money." He leaned back in his chair. "Times were hard, Pavel Andreievich. My mother was a widow on a pension that barely kept her alive, and my brother Misha was still in school. I did what I had to do to help them, and when Misha was out of school—" Glakov looked away for a moment. "I decided to leave Earth when a friend informed me that the authorities wanted to detain me for questioning."

Chekov finished his tea. "That does not quite explain all of the stories I was told."

Glakov spread his hands, palms up. "I am afraid that I often told Misha exaggerated tales of my exploits. I didn't do that solely to make myself more important in his eyes, I did it so that he would believe that he had a brother able to protect him from harm and would not worry as much about his safety and that of our mother. And then I was gone before he could find out the truth."

Chekov was silent.

"Please, Pavel Andreievich—you must tell me what happened to Misha in later years. Your comrade Farley

Longstreet has already briefed us on some of Earth's history—I know about World War III."

"Your brother did not survive it," Chekov replied, "but he had three children who did."

Glakov sighed. "He has been dead all these years. I have known that had to be so for some time now, and yet to hear this from you—"

"You have been through much hardship, Dmitri Sergeievich," Chekov said, feeling how inadequate his words were.

"Yes. More than perhaps you can understand. You are looking at a man who gave up all hope some time ago, when we knew that our ship's drive was failing. You are looking at a man who believed that he and his comrades would never arrive at the world they sought, who saw friends dying aboard a vessel that he believed would inevitably become a mass grave. You are looking at one who felt his body failing him, growing weaker every hour. I did not consider suicide, for I was already dead. And now you and your crewmates have resurrected me." The older man paused. "I think that to understand what we went through, you would have to read some of the works of our country's great writer Dostoyevsky, if any record of them still exists."

"His works have survived, my kinsman," Chekov said, "and I have read them."

"You will forgive me." Glakov got to his feet. "Your physicians are skilled healers, but I have grown fatigued now, and must rest some more."

"Of course." Chekov was still wondering if he could believe everything his ancestor had told him.

* * *

16

Leander Cortés was sitting up on a biobed, getting scanned by Dr. McCoy, when Kirk entered sickbay. Several other people from the *Hawking* lay on beds near their captain. A few people were resting; others held small portable viewscreens. Chekov's relative, Dmitri Glakov, sat at a small table playing chess with another man. A woman on a biobed in one corner was talking to Ilsa Soong.

During the week that Cortés's people had been aboard, Kirk had familiarized himself with the names of most of them. That tall pale man gazing intently at his small viewscreen was Emo Tannan, the *Hawking*'s first officer, while the woman with the long black braid talking to Dr. Soong was Rachel Zlatopolsky, an engineer. The short bearded man playing chess with Glakov was Nasser al-Aswari. All of them looked healthier, and would soon be strong enough to discuss their future, but Kirk noticed the wariness in their faces as he crossed the room.

"Greetings, Captain Cortés," Kirk said. The commander of the *Hawking* looked rested, his lean face was filling out, and his gray hair had been trimmed to collar length, but he still seemed nervous. Cortés shifted uneasily on his bed and eyed McCoy's medical tricorder as if he expected the instrument to turn on him.

"Heart rate's normal," McCoy said as he passed the tricorder over Cortés's chest. "Bone density's returning to normal." He glanced at Kirk. "What brings you here, Jim?"

"I just wanted to see how our guests were doing." Kirk glanced back at the others in sickbay. They were all watching him now. The youngest of the group in this area

17

of sickbay were two people in their late forties, while all the others were in their fifties and sixties; there were no people younger or older than that from the *Hawking*. In a few weeks, they would be fully recovered, feeling as though they were again in the prime of life. He wondered if they would be able to accept that fact.

He turned toward Cortés and McCoy. "I trust, Captain Cortés, that you are feeling much better," Kirk said.

Cortés leaned forward slightly. "Yes, I am. It's quite remarkable that your medical treatments work so swiftly. I had thought that I would never feel well again."

McCoy cleared his throat. "And you're going to be feeling even better in a few days."

Cortés shook his head. "Remarkable."

"We'll be holding meetings soon," Kirk said, "so that you and all of your crewmates can start making some decisions."

McCoy nodded. "And we'll all be looking forward to hearing more about your voyage, about its beginnings and its goals."

Kirk realized instantly what Bones was trying to do: get Cortés to look past his fears and suffering by preparing to talk about his ordeal. It was an old-fashioned ploy, but sometimes effective. Kirk was of the view that putting people into a new environment where they would have to function in fresh ways was a more plausible therapy; but until the *Enterprise* deposited these people in their new home, McCoy's gentle prodding would probably do no harm. Kirk reminded himself again that he still knew little about these people. It wouldn't hurt to ferret more information out of them before any meetings took place.

Leander Cortés took a deep breath; for several long moments, he was silent, seemingly unwilling or unable to speak.

"I don't mean to pry," McCoy said, "but I thought it might help—"

"That's all right, Doctor." Cortés rested his hands on his knees. "We left a choking, damaged Earth, only to face the problems of a confined ecology aboard our ship." He paused and looked around the infirmary, as if trying to make up his mind how to continue.

Kirk waited.

"The plan, upon reaching our new world," Cortés went on, "was to bring forth children from the protected genetic material stored aboard our ship. But of course that became an increasingly distant goal after we realized that the *Hawking* was slowing down. Some of us might have decided to have children on board, but that prospect became an unacceptable horror as time dragged on and our ecosystems developed problems of infestation and disease. We could not condemn innocent children to such a life, to such constricted and hazardous circumstances. Twenty-five of our comrades died before we were able to bring the most virulent viruses and bacteria under control. It was not the best ship that we started with, but it was the best we could get. We were fortunate to have a ship at all."

"Lieutenant Longstreet tells me that it was quite a sophisticated vessel for its time," Kirk said. The *Hawking* was equipped with a quantum gravitational-impulse power drive that drew its energy from the vacuum flux.

"It obviously wasn't sophisticated enough to keep from breaking down," Cortés said.

"When Mr. Spock first scanned your ship," Kirk continued, "he mentioned that the sensor readings indicated that the *Hawking* apparently ran into at least one flux dead spot in the vacuum. That would have been enough to have erroneously convinced you that there was something wrong with the drive itself, when it was only a dead spot in the field. A century from now, your drive would have cut in again."

"That would have been too late for us."

"True," McCoy said, "but you couldn't have been expected to know that its failure was the result of that kind of problem. After all, you—"

"Yes, Doctor, I know," Cortés muttered. "I am only an ignorant man from a time long past, from a world that no longer exists as I knew it." He fell silent, as if suddenly aware that he might be revealing too much.

Kirk thought of what Chekov had told him about his kinsman Glakov. Perhaps only a petty criminal, or possibly a man guilty of serious crimes—they had no way of knowing what was true about the man, and the same doubts could be applied to everyone from the *Hawking*.

"What, Captain," Kirk said, "were your specific reasons for leaving Earth?"

Cortés shifted on the biobed, clearly reluctant to reply.

"Let me assure you," Kirk continued, "as I have before, that there is nothing from today's Earth that can do you and your people any harm, or which has any authority to hold you accountable for any old wrongs."

Cortés drew his brows together. "We disapproved of the Earth we left behind, Captain Kirk. Most of us knew, for one reason or another, that there was no future for any of us there. That is about all I have to tell you at the moment."

"As you wish," Kirk said, "but rest assured that Earth now is a much, much better place than the one you left behind. You've all had a chance to learn a little about what's happened there since you left, and Lieutenant Longstreet will be happy to answer any of your questions."

"Oh, I'm sure he will," Emo Tannan said from behind Kirk, and the captain heard a tone of sarcasm and bitterness in the man's voice.

"Jim, let me finish my examination of this man." McCoy studied his tricorder readings. "No more signs of that respiratory infection you had when you came aboard, Captain Cortés. You've completely recovered from that."

Cortés grimaced. "Considering the ecological difficulties of long-term life aboard our ship," he said, "it's a wonder we didn't develop much more virulent infections. Of course our ailments and diseases were only one of our problems. We also had the psychological problems of long confinement, to which was added the distress of realizing that our drive was failing. And as we slowly gave up any hope of arrival, of settling our new world and populating it with children, we became increasingly conscious of what we had become—prisoners, condemned to incarceration with no hope of escape."

Now that he was talking more freely, Cortés seemed unable to stop himself. "We grew closer to one another," he went on, "and then more suspicious of one another, and not a day passed without my worrying that someone would suddenly lapse into insanity, fall into complete

21

catatonia, or commit suicide. I would make secret bets with myself about who might be the first to succumb, as I suspect all of us did from time to time. And I would wonder what the first suicide or the first person to slip into derangement would do to the rest of us. We grew more strange, and more suspicious, and more fearful of saying or doing anything that might trigger any of our shipmates, and that is what you see in us today."

Kirk found himself moved by the older man's words. Science and technology had left the people of the *Hawking* behind. When they had come out of the solar system, it was to fulfill a yearning for a better place among the stars, away from the turmoil of their home world. Their dream was not unlike the impulse that had created the Federation, Starfleet, and the *Enterprise*. Cortés and his people might have their greatest difficulty in accepting the enormity of the social progress that had occurred since their flight from Earth, in knowing that a better life awaited them wherever they might wish to settle. They had been without hope, and now they had prospects beyond anything they had envisioned. That might be enough to unhinge many of them.

"What shall become of us now?" someone called out.

Kirk turned and saw that all of the others near him had been listening to Cortés.

"Will you take us to our destination?" Rachel Zlatopolsky said from the other end of the room. "Or are we to be returned to Earth?"

"We should know shortly," Kirk replied, "whether there is a suitable world at your original destination star."

"We had every reason to think that there would be a

habitable planet there," Emo Tannan said from his bed. "But maybe you think of us as much too primitive to have ascertained that before setting out."

"The suitability of your destination isn't all that we have to verify, Mr. Tannan," Kirk said, ignoring the sarcasm. "We are checking not only to make sure that there is an Earthlike world in that system, but also whether or not it already has a colony or has a claim on it that the Federation is bound to honor."

Cortés shook his head. "Of course. Faster ships. . . ."

"We expect to have more information in a few days, perhaps sooner," Kirk continued, "and we'll let you know immediately what we find out."

McCoy frowned. "In the meantime," he murmured, "your best course of action is to recover and rebuild your strength, and not worry about the decisions you'll be making later on." The doctor gazed pointedly at Kirk.

Cortés sighed. "I can tell you that at least some of my people, beaten down by what we've all endured, may very well ask to return to Earth, especially if—as you say—it is now a better place. We'll have to wait and see if the desire to settle a new world still exists in any of us."

"That," McCoy said, "will only become apparent when you have all regained your full health and strength. Tired bodies and minds don't hope very well."

"Hope!" Emo Tannan almost spat the word. "I gave up on that long ago. Better to accept our hell and give up the habit of hoping."

Nasser al-Aswari turned around in his chair. "Some of us may want to see our old home again," the bearded man said, "if it exists, if what you're saying about it is the truth."

23

Kirk folded his arms. "I'll be very direct with all of you. Earth isn't anything like the place you knew—psychologically, it may be too disorienting for you. Maybe later, after a few years of life on a colony world that could give you something like the life you expected to have when you started on your voyage, it might become possible for some of you to visit Earth. Some of your children may choose to go there eventually."

"I see what you're saying," Rachel Zlatopolsky muttered from her bed. "We'd be obsolete. Everything we would hope to see is long gone, and everyone we knew there is dead. It might be too wrenching to endure."

"You may be wrong, Rachel," Dmitri Glakov called out as he looked up from his chessboard. "I have discovered a kinsman of mine aboard this vessel, so I suspect that there are still some in my homeland who would know of me!"

A few people laughed, but uneasily.

"Jim," McCoy said, "you'll be holding meetings with these folks soon enough. You're not going to start holding them in sickbay. Time to let my patients get some of the rest they still need."

"All right, Bones." Kirk nodded briefly at Cortés, then moved toward the nearest exit. He felt the eyes of the *Hawking*'s people on him before the door slid shut behind him.

Spock sat at his station on the bridge, having finished his review of the rest of the data. He had attended all of the meetings Captain Kirk had been holding with small groups from the *Hawking*, observing how gratified the captain was by the reactions of the exiles from Earth. Word had spread to the other passengers after the first meeting, as Captain Kirk had known it would, so that each successive meeting had something to build on. Each group of people, Spock had noticed, seemed a little stronger, more willing to express their thoughts, more able to consider and discuss their future plans rationally.

As health had returned to Leander Cortés's people, larger numbers of them had shown an increasing desire to go on to the star that was their original destination, to complete the original goal of their costly venture by settling a habitable world in that system. Cortés had told both Spock and Kirk only the day before that a majority of the *Hawking*'s people now favored that option.

Unfortunate, Spock thought, that they would now be unable to carry out their plan.

He touched a communicator panel next to the display screen. "Captain," he said, "may I request that you come to the bridge?"

"Kirk here," the captain's voice replied. "I'm on my way. What is it, Spock?"

"I now have all the information we were seeking about the *Hawking*'s destination star."

Kirk had asked Leander Cortés and his people to meet him in the large briefing room near the gymnasium. All of them were waiting for him when he entered the room, trailed by Spock, McCoy, and Soong.

Most of them had found chairs; others stood on either side of the room against the walls. Cortés sat with Emo Tannan on the raised platform at the other end of the room. Kirk went to them, hurried up the two steps to the stage, then turned to face the gathering.

"Friends," Kirk said, "I have an announcement to make." Expectant, hopeful eyes watched him. He glanced at Ilsa Soong, thinking of what she had told him earlier; these people, despite the great improvement in their health and well-being, were still in a fragile emotional state. Even so, there was no point in lying to them, in trying to save them this additional blow. Even if he had been able to get away with lying, he and his crew had worked too hard to win the trust of these people to attempt to deceive them now.

"Our destination," Cortés said. "That's why you've called us all here, isn't it? You've finally found out what we need to know."

"Yes," Kirk said. "I'm sorry to report that your destination star has no Earthlike planets—no planets at all, in fact. Commander Spock has confirmed this. There is no doubt."

There was a long silence. No one moved; no one even seemed to be breathing.

"But how can this be?" Cortés said at last. "We had every indication . . . our data. . . ." He shook his head. "We would never have set off in complete ignorance of what we could expect."

Kirk looked into the eyes of the people nearest the platform, and realized that they would now have to accept that their sacrifice had been in vain, that all their decades of suffering would have led them only to a desert, an empty space.

"I can't believe it," Emo Tannan muttered. "Our drive

fails because of something we couldn't have known about, a dead spot in our drive's field. Now we find out that there wasn't anything in the place where we were headed. Our lives were wasted—we threw them away for nothing. We would have done better to stay on Earth and—"

"Emo," Cortés said softly, and the other man fell silent.

Kirk had to tell them the rest of the story, whatever fears that might stir in them. "Your data were not mistaken," he said. "Your information was correct—there was a planetary system there, including an Earthlike world, but all of those planets were destroyed by an alien mechanism, a giant thing that ate planets for fuel."

"What?" Cortés asked.

"That is the fact," Spock said as he stepped onto the platform. "We managed to stop the intruder after it had eaten other systems. This mechanism was apparently an instrumentality left over from an ancient conflict, and it was the Federation's misfortune that it came into our sector of the galaxy. One cannot ascribe any animosity to this device's actions. It had to consume matter to survive."

"And it isn't a threat any more," Kirk said quickly. "It was stopped. We destroyed the thing. A brave man named Commodore Matthew Decker gave his life to stop it. The ship's computer has our record of the encounter if you wish to reassure yourselves about its outcome."

Cortés sank back in his chair. "This is still terrifying news."

"But at least you know now that your original plan was not mistaken," Kirk said. "There might have been a world

27

for you in that system. There would have been, except for that alien berserker."

"We would have got where we were going if our ship's engine hadn't developed problems we couldn't foresee, and were too ignorant to repair," Tannan said. "We would have had a world to settle if some damned planet-eater hadn't gobbled it up. How many other things that we can't possibly know about are lying in wait for us?"

"Perhaps," Cortés said in a firm voice, "given what Captain Kirk has just told us, we should be grateful that our ship's engines did fail, and that we didn't arrive at our destination sooner."

The other captain was also trying to put the best face on the news, Kirk realized. The people looking to him still seemed stunned; this was simply too much for them to take in right away. Reactions of dismay, disappointment, and even dread and despair would set in later, and some of those feelings would take root, unless steps were taken quickly to prevent it.

"Let me say something," McCoy said as he joined Kirk and the others on the stage. Kirk saw that Bones had the matter in hand, and knew what to say now. These people might have more trust in the words of the man who had restored them all to health.

"What can you possibly have to say?" Nasser al-Aswari shouted, but the people sitting near him were already motioning to him to be quiet.

"Captain Kirk would not have come here," McCoy continued, "only to give you bad news and destroy your hopes. Starfleet has informed us that there is a suitable planet in a nearby system where you can settle, if you wish. A colony from Earth was established there forty years ago, and we've been told that it's willing to accept new settlers. You'd have some of the advantages of our present technology, but without the extreme disorientation you'd suffer on Earth. You could choose to live among the people already there, or go off and found your own settlement. Of course, there are also other possibilities—this is only one you might wish to consider."

"You don't have to decide this now," Kirk cut in. "Think about it, talk it over, but you should know this—Starfleet and the Federation look out for our member worlds and allies in what is often a dangerous galaxy. As we look outward, it may get even more dangerous, but you've all faced danger already. You were willing to risk the unknown." He paused. "Your ship isn't the first from the past that we've discovered, and it may not be the last. We might need your help in times to come, or the help of your children, in assisting other voyagers to adapt to new circumstances. Your perspectives will be useful and valuable."

After a moment, Captain Cortés got to his feet and came to Kirk's side. "Thank you for your reassuring words," Cortés said.

"They're more than that," Kirk replied. "They are a pledge."

"I take your meaning." Cortés looked out at his shipmates. "We have much to consider now."

Kirk thought of the S.S. *Botany Bay*, another vessel from Earth's past, whose encounter with the *Enterprise* had not been as peaceful or as productive as this one promised to be. He did not have to fear that Leander

Cortés would try to take over his ship, as Khan Noonien Singh had tried to do. The future of Khan's people on the world where they had been exiled, Ceti Alpha V, was still to be decided. A piece of a violent past had been tied off in that encounter, as one might tie off a severed limb; but Kirk was determined to find a better fate for the people from the *Hawking*.

Chapter Four

MONTGOMERY SCOTT stood near the stern of the *Hawking* in front of a metal wall discolored by greenish stains, scanning the area in front of him with his tricorder and trying to ignore the smell of the place. Mr. Spock, who had beamed aboard with him and Farley Longstreet, peered at the readings on his own tricorder.

"Wow," Longstreet muttered, "does it ever reek in here. As somebody from Cortés's time might have put it, this ship smells like a locker room after the big game. Maybe we should have brought along some noseplugs."

Scotty wrinkled his nose, then studied his tricorder readings, knowing what they were likely to tell him while still hoping that he might be wrong.

"There is definitely a weapon behind that wall and the shielding," Mr. Spock murmured.

"Aye," Scotty said, "there's no doubt about it now."

"It was unlikely," Spock said, "that scanning this part

of the ship at close range would contradict what we found in our analysis of our earlier scan."

Scotty sighed. "With something this worrisome, better to leave no doubt. Now that we know for certain that the old wreck is carrying a thermonuclear bomb, I just canna understand why Captain Cortés never said anything about it to us." Cortés and his people, Scotty thought, might not be so harmless as they had at first seemed.

"I'm surprised at that, too," Longstreet said. "Cortés doesn't strike me as a devious man. Still, given the troubled world he came from, maybe he felt the need to pack some heat, as another idiom of his time would have phrased it."

"Captain Cortés knows that the *Enterprise*'s technology is far more advanced than that of the *Hawking*," Spock said. "He might have kept his silence in the beginning when he was uncertain of our intentions, but he is surely aware by now that we are capable of scanning his ship thoroughly. He would know, or at least guess, that he could not have kept this kind of secret indefinitely, so perhaps he concluded that there was no need to tell us about what he had aboard."

Scotty shook his head. "You're cutting the man a lot of slack, Mr. Spock. I'm starting to wonder if we should have been more cautious about bringing those people aboard." He slipped his tricorder under his belt. "We'd best be getting back to the *Enterprise*. We'll have to tell the captain what we've found right away."

Kirk was just finishing his workout on one of the running platforms when Leonard McCoy and Ilsa Soong came into the gymnasium. They wore loose shirts and pants, obviously prepared for a workout of their own. As Kirk stepped away from the running platform, McCoy leaned past him to look at the gauges on the machine's handrail.

"The usual slow, steady, strong heart rate," McCoy said. "Well, Jim, I guess I won't have to prescribe more exercise for you or haul you in for another examination just yet."

Kirk smiled and reached for a towel. "Physician, heal thyself," he said.

"That's the reason we're here," Dr. Soong said, "to get some exercise. We've been so preoccupied with our new patients that we're in danger of neglecting our own physical health."

"The more time I spend with Cortés and his people," McCoy said, "the more I'm convinced that to put them on a planet where they would be the only colonists is not a good idea. After the decades of isolation on their ship, they should become part of a larger community."

"They've begun to adapt to being around us," Soong added, "and that's a good sign. To be isolated again might leave them even worse off psychologically than before."

"A place like Merope Four would be much better for them," McCoy continued. Merope IV was the planet Starfleet had recommended for Cortés and his people, but Kirk knew there was no point in contacting its governing body directly and making any plans until the refugees from the *Hawking* had decided what to do. "Since the colony has only about two hundred and fifty thousand people, most of them living in smaller settlements, our people wouldn't feel lost there."

Kirk nodded as he wiped his face with the towel, noting the acceptance of responsibility that went with the doctor's use of the words "our people." The information Starfleet had sent about Merope IV had told them that it was an Earthlike world with three large continents. The two smaller continents, New Yoruba and New Biafra, lay in the northern hemisphere and were still unsettled by human beings, while the largest continent, New Niger, was south of the equator and home to the Federation colonists who had settled there. All of the land masses had large forests and a temperate climate, with average temperatures ranging from zero degrees to twenty-five degrees Centigrade.

Perhaps more important, in Kirk's opinion, was that the native flora of Merope IV was much like that of Earth's temperate regions, and that the native animals included creatures resembling Earth's deer, moose, wolves, bears, birds, and waterfowl. That would make it somewhat easier for Cortés and his comrades to adapt.

"Uhura and Longstreet," Kirk said, "are already putting together a presentation on Merope Four for our guests, so that they can consider whether or not to settle there."

"From what we know already, Merope Four sounds ideal," McCoy said. "It should present challenges to human settlers without being overly harsh or inhospitable. It'll almost be familiar."

Kirk nodded. "And most of the other possible colonies have two drawbacks," he said. "They're either so large and well established that the *Hawking*'s people will feel disoriented and lost in the crowd, or in such early stages of settlement that they might feel too isolated again."

McCoy stepped onto the moving surface of the running platform, gripped the handrail, and began his warmup. "Helping build a new settlement," the chief physician said, "with recently arrived settlers and their children is the best mental therapy I can think of. And nothing will prevent them from traveling to Earth at some future time, if that's what they want to do."

Ilsa Soong chuckled. "I think that's exactly what Ensign Chekov's kinsman Dmitri Glakov is hoping to do in time."

The doors to the gym opened again; Spock and Scotty came into the room, followed by Farley Longstreet. "Captain," Scotty called out, "we've just beamed back from the *Hawking*. There's something you should know about that old ship."

"As it happens," Kirk said, "we were just in the middle of discussing our guests. Bones and Ilsa both think Merope Four would be a good home for them."

Spock lifted a brow. "I would anticipate," the Vulcan said, "that not all of Captain Cortés's people will be at peace with a decision to go to Merope Four or to any other colonized planet."

"Are you certain, Mr. Spock?" Soong asked. "My impression is that most of them are now leaning toward settling a world that already has a colony."

"Spock," Kirk said, "what evidence do you have for your . . . can we call them suspicions?"

"I do have evidence for my suppositions," Spock said,

"but I must caution that it is ambiguous, and perhaps irrelevant."

Scotty shook his head. "Let's just say that what we found out raises some doubts about our guests."

McCoy released the handrail and stepped off the running platform; a frown crossed his face. Kirk folded his arms. "What is it?" Kirk asked.

Spock said, "A careful examination of our previous scan of the *Hawking* revealed that the old starship is carrying a thermonuclear bomb. Mr. Scott thought it advisable, if admittedly somewhat redundant, to beam aboard Captain Cortés's ship with Mr. Longstreet and me to confirm those findings, so that there can be no doubt. The weapon is heavily shielded, apparently not so much to protect the *Hawking*'s passengers from its dangers as to hide it from detection. Our sensors of course detected its presence, but according to Lieutenant Longstreet, a more primitive technology, one from Captain Cortés's time, probably would not have found it."

Kirk pressed his lips together. There might be no reason to be suspicious of Captain Cortés and his people, but how could that be tested? He thought of Khan Noonien Singh, and the damage and terror he might have inflicted on others with the *Enterprise* under his control, had Kirk not succeeded in recapturing his ship.

"Mr. Longstreet," Kirk said, turning toward the young historian, "you probably know more about the technology of Cortés's time than most of us. Can you think of any innocuous reason for a ship of that time to be carrying a thermonuclear device?"

Farley Longstreet shook his head. "In a word, no. A

fission-fusion pulse engine on an interplanetary vessel—
that I might expect, or some other sort of nuclear-powered
engine, but not something that's obviously a weapon—not
unless, of course, it's a military ship."

Ilsa Soong frowned. "And none of our patients
breathed a word of this to us—I can assure you of that."

"They might not have felt the need to say anything,"
McCoy said, "given the violent century from which
they've come."

"Yes," Longstreet said, "and their bomb is a reminder
of that time."

Kirk realized then what he would have to do. "I'll
speak with Cortés privately, and ask him what he expects
us to do with his ship. If he says we should abandon it,
we'll know the bomb means nothing, and I'll simply ask
him to tell me more about it. But if he indicates that he
wishes his ship to be taken in tow, I'll confront him about
the purpose of his hidden weapon."

Kirk stood with Leander Cortés and Christine Chapel
at the entrance to the hangar deck and shuttlebay. He had
asked the captain of the *Hawking* to meet him here, not
wanting to confront him aggressively with what he now
knew.

Whatever suspicions knowledge of the bomb had
roused in him, Kirk reminded himself that Cortés was a
voyager from the heroic age of space travel. Although
only thirty years had passed for him and his crew in relative time, they had spent almost two centuries of crawling
across this segment of the galaxy to their destination. The
captain of the *Hawking* and his shipmates had obeyed the

known Einsteinian science of their day and, following its restrictions, they had expended whatever energy was necessary to accomplish their journey.

As Spock had put it to Kirk during one of their talks, "The physical discovery that fast-moving clocks run slow might even be described as a mercy to human aspirations. That mercy written into physical law said that if you want star travel badly enough, then there is this one way to pay for it." The people aboard the *Hawking* had paid that human cost, while future generations had gone on to circumvent Einstein.

Weakened by their long voyage, perhaps believing themselves near death . . . Cortés and his people had been incapable then of any aggressive acts against Kirk and his crew. Captain Cortés was also an intelligent man who had probably learned enough about the *Enterprise* and its personnel by now to realize that trying to seize the starship would be a fool's game. Despite his earlier experience with Khan Noonien Singh and the people of the *Botany Bay,* Kirk did not actually believe that Cortés and his people were a threat to him. Even the brilliant and extremely formidable Khan had needed the aid—the insubordination—of one of Kirk's own officers, Lieutenant Marla McGivers, to temporarily take over the *Enterprise.*

But Cortés's weapon could be a threat to a colony world like Merope IV, once the *Enterprise* was gone from that space.

"There's a sight that should reassure you, Captain," Kirk said to the other man as he gestured at the shuttle-craft bay. "I know some of your people are still nervous about our transporters. It might be more cumbersome and time-consuming to transport your more apprehensive comrades in shuttlecraft to their eventual destination, but we can manage it if necessary."

"We've all been through the transporters once," Cortés said, "when you . . . er . . . beamed us aboard. I think we can all steel ourselves to use them again. In any case, I'm not so sure that giving us all a tour of the shuttlebay would necessarily be reassuring, since the presence of these craft implies that your transporters don't always work."

"I won't claim that they don't occasionally malfunction," Kirk said, "but that's not anything you have to worry about under normal circumstances. We have shuttlecraft aboard largely because of the limits on the range of our transporters."

"If you gentlemen will excuse me," Nurse Chapel said, "I'm needed back in sickbay." She glanced at Cortés. "Think you can find your way back?"

"I think so," Cortés replied.

Chapel left them as the two men walked through the entrance. The crewmembers on hangar duty greeted their captain and saluted the man from the past as Kirk led Cortés around the deck, pointing out various features of the craft; the *Hawking*'s captain seemed fascinated by every detail of the *Enterprise*. Kirk had already spent a fair amount of time with Cortés, and the man did not strike him as either dangerous or deceptive. The *Enterprise*'s crew would have made little progress in winning the trust of the *Hawking*'s people without Cortés's example. At every meeting, the *Hawking*'s captain had done his best to be constructive and helpful. Kirk's instincts were still telling him that he could trust the other man.

"I didn't ask you to come here only for a tour of the hangar," Kirk said. "I also wanted to tell you that Starfleet has strongly recommended that you and your people consider settling on a colony world called Merope Four. The people there are willing—indeed anxious—to welcome new settlers. Naturally, all of you will be given information about that planet, and any decision will be up to you."

"I suppose we'll have to have more meetings, then."

"Dr. McCoy and Dr. Soong think you should again meet with your people in small groups, but perhaps without my presence or the presence of any of my crew this time. Your people shouldn't feel that we're trying to force any particular decision on you."

"You've been extremely sensitive to our . . . predicament," Cortés said, and Kirk heard the sincerity in his voice. "It must have been difficult to deal with people who have become so . . . inward." He looked up. "But we're beginning to look outside ourselves again."

"Captain Cortés," Kirk said, "I have a question to ask you. Three of my officers, Commander Spock among them, have informed me that your ship is carrying a thermonuclear bomb, shielded in an attempt to prevent its detection." The other man was still gazing at him steadily. "Why are you carrying such a weapon?"

"Part of the *Hawking* was once an old military ship called the *Aleksandr Lebed*. We had to retrofit it to make it into a starship."

"Why didn't you disarm the weapon?" Kirk asked.

Cortés shrugged. "To be honest, we didn't know how."

Kirk tried to muster more suspicion, but Cortés had the

40

demeanor of a man willing to answer his questions honestly. "You were able to take an interplanetary ship and turn it into an interstellar vessel?"

"Not quite," Cortés said. "The *Hawking* was actually put together from two smaller vessels, the *Lebed* and a civilian craft, the *Victoria*. Or rather, that work was done for us by people we hired. To get rid of the bomb altogether would have cost us more than we could afford, and our resources were limited."

"But still you didn't think to disarm the bomb."

"We made no effort to hide it. Given what I've seen of your technology, I was almost certain you'd detect it sooner or later." Cortés leaned against a shuttlecraft. "Captain, the bomb isn't armed. It's there, but it's basically useless."

"How can you know that?" Kirk asked.

"We have no control panel for it anywhere I've been able to find. You can check that for yourselves. Ask my chief engineer, Rachel Zlatopolsky—she'll tell you the same thing."

"Why didn't you mention the bomb to us earlier?"

"It didn't seem important," Cortés answered. "It's like an old electrical connection that no longer goes anywhere in a house, since it's disconnected from both the power source and an outlet. Sooner or later, it's noticed, and you've noticed it. What more can I say?"

Kirk was trying hard to be suspicious of the old Earthman, but his story was plausible.

"You're welcome to disarm the bomb," Cortés continued. "You'd surely find it simple enough to do so."

"And what would you like us to do with your ship?" Kirk asked carefully.

"Personally, Captain," Cortés said, "I don't much care. I'd be willing to leave it behind, assuming that the bomb is disarmed and doesn't pose any threat to any future voyager who might come upon it. But some of my people have an attachment to what you might call their place of agony, I suppose. There are also things we have aboard, personal items and artifacts and the like, that we would want to keep with us. Would it be possible for you to take the *Hawking* in tow to our eventual destination?"

Kirk nodded. His intellectual suspicions were rising once more, but his emotions told him to trust Cortés.

"If you defuse the bomb," Cortés went on, "assuming that's necessary, there shouldn't be anything for you to worry about."

Kirk thought of what Scotty had said before they had left the gymnasium: Don't simply defuse the bomb. Get rid of the blasted thing altogether.

Kirk shook his head. "With or without the bomb, we still may not be able to tow your ship that far, not with the drive you have. Even if we repaired it, the *Hawking* would take many years to get to any nearby Federation world at its relativistic sublight speed. Couldn't we simply remove anything your people wish to take along?"

"Of course we could," Cortés murmured, "if that isn't too much trouble for you, and you have the space."

"To get the *Hawking* to a colony nearby, to Merope Four for example, would probably require that we attach a small warp engine to it, or take the ship in tow by attaching it to the *Enterprise*. Mr. Scott and his engineers would have to work out how it might be done and whether or not it's feasible."

Cortés sighed. "I understand—thoughtless of me not to consider the cost to you. I suppose it would be an expensive proposition."

"Oh, no." Kirk shook his head. "Not really. Federation economics can afford just about any expenditure of power. This isn't a budgetary problem—we don't have a money system as you did."

Cortés smiled. "Then you must be rich beyond imagining."

It was Kirk's turn to smile. "You can put it that way. Let's just say that scarcity doesn't govern our sense of values. What I need to know is whether the *Hawking* is necessary to the lives of your people. If it is, we'll do what's needed." He now knew that he trusted the man.

"And the bomb?"

"We'll disarm it," Kirk said, "if it needs to be disarmed. But we might as well leave it aboard. Its design, and the materials used in constructing it, may be of interest to our engineers and my science officer."

Cortés gazed at him steadily. "I am very grateful for your show of trust, Captain Kirk. It tells me much about the kind of society you come from, and its difference from the world we left so long ago."

"The *Hawking* does have historical and technical interest," Kirk said, "so it should be preserved until we've learned what we can, at least until we get as far as Merope Four, if that's where your people decide they want to go."

"Do give us all the information you can about the place. Personally, my feeling is that if your Starfleet thinks it's a good place for us, then we probably ought to go there. I'm assuming that your psychology and sociology are the equivalent of your advanced technology."

"Do you think your people would prefer to arrive in their own ship," Kirk asked, "or aboard the *Enterprise?*"

"That's something we'll have to discuss at our meetings," Cortés said, "along with the possible merits of becoming new settlers on Merope Four. We have a lot of decisions to make, Captain. Thank you for offering us the choice."

Montgomery Scott was still tinkering with a console that needed repairs as Kirk finished explaining what he wanted the engineering crew to do. The captain suppressed a smile as Scotty shook his head in irritation and finally looked up at him. Good old Scotty, Kirk thought. His hands were always busy; he was a man who loved his job.

Scotty glanced at Spock, then turned back to Kirk. "Not meaning to question orders, sir," the chief engineer said, "but the last time I looked, there was plenty of room—unless we're hauling cargo I don't know about. It would be a lot simpler just to take everyone aboard the *Enterprise.*" Lieutenant Ivan Darmer, the engineering officer standing next to Scotty, nodded in agreement.

Kirk sighed. "Scotty, it's their pride. After all the years, they have to get where they're going in their own ship, if that's possible." The engineer regarded his captain silently for a moment, and Kirk saw that Scotty understood.

"Then we'll do our best to accommodate them," Scotty said.

"Can you set up a tow brace?" Kirk asked.

Scotty folded his arms. "Well, it's a wee bit easier than rigging their ship with a warp engine. But if they're going to travel in the *Hawking,* we'll also have to fix their environmental systems. You wouldna believe how much the old wreck stinks."

"Do it," Kirk said.

"The *Hawking,*" Spock said, "and even the bomb aboard it, do have some historical technical interest. The ship should not be destroyed, at least not yet."

Scotty nodded. "I take all of your points. I'll rig up the tow brace and work with them to set up their environment to last until we get to Merope Four, at least."

"How long will it take?" Kirk asked.

Scotty glanced at Lieutenant Darmer, obviously considering the question. "I canna be sure, but I'll estimate we could make her fit in a week."

"Then I'll tell Dr. McCoy that everyone who is in good enough shape, and who would like to leave, be allowed to go back to the *Hawking.*"

Scotty shook his head. "Captain, that ship is such an old hulk, and so wrecked inside, that it pains me to see her try to go on in the state she's in."

Kirk smiled. "Just fix her so she can last as far as Merope Four. We'll have to see if she can serve beyond that point."

"Aye," Scotty said. "It hurts to see how backward she is, and all the wounds she has, but we'll do our best."

Kirk left engineering, with Spock at his side. As the door closed behind them, Kirk murmured to the science officer, "I'll bet he falls in love with the old hulk yet."

* * *

Rachel Zlatopolsky had requested permission to come back aboard the *Enterprise* and make her report to Montgomery Scott directly. Scotty met her in the transporter room and ushered her to the lift that would take them to the engineering deck. The engineer could have spoken to him from the *Hawking,* but he knew why she wanted to meet with him face to face. It was part of her pride, working with him as an equal and giving him her reports in person. She was also proving to him, and perhaps to herself, that she and most of her crewmates were getting over their fear of the transporter.

And, Scotty admitted to himself, he did not at all mind having Rachel's company. Once she had recovered from her astonishment at the *Enterprise*'s technical capacities, she had been anxious to learn everything she could about the starship. Her advice about the specific weaknesses and failures of the *Hawking*'s environmental systems had been extremely useful in repairing them. Rachel was also, in her state of restored health and vigor, quite bonny; the skin of her handsome fine-boned face was smoother and less wrinkled, and there were hardly any silver strands of hair in her long black braid now.

"All of our life-support systems are in working order now," she said to him as they left the lift and entered main engineering. "We finally got rid of the smell. Our only remaining minor problem is some mildew in a couple of the showers." Almost all of the people of the *Hawking* were back on board their own ship, and most of them had spent the past week doing whatever they could to help Scotty and his engineers repair and refurbish the old craft, as if their own regained health had resulted in a greater need to bring their vessel back to order. Many of them, including Rachel, had gone out of their way to do the messier jobs of ripping out old wires and cleaning out the waste conduits.

Scotty himself had been much more amenable to working on the old hulk after he had checked the nuclear weapon in its central vault of concealment and had confirmed that the bomb had in fact never been armed. There had also been some personal gratification for him in supervising the repairs, in seeing the old hulk become shipshape. He could trust her to get to Merope IV now while keeping her passengers safe.

A viewscreen to Rachel's right showed an image of the *Hawking,* now held below the *Enterprise* by a tractor beam. She stopped to gaze at the screen for a moment. "Mr. Scott," she said, "I might as well tell you that most of us have decided to settle on Merope Four, and even those who have expressed some doubts about that would still rather stay with the rest of us than go off on their own. Leander Cortés will deliver that news to Captain Kirk himself in a few hours."

"You're sure?" Scotty said.

"We're sure. After reviewing all the information, I doubt we could do better, and—" A smile flickered across her face. "It will be wonderful to feel ground under my feet again, and breathe fresh air."

Scotty looked at the image on the screen. "The *Hawking* is such a direct piece of design," he said. "Why, it's almost shameful in its reliable simplicity."

"It did the job of keeping us alive," Rachel said.

"Aye," Scotty replied, "that it did, lassie . . . er, Rachel."

She turned toward him.

"I'll listen to your report, and then perhaps we can be on our way to the mess for a wee celebration."

Rachel's dark eyes widened. "A celebration, Mr. Scott . . . um, Scotty?"

"Marking this new phase of your journey to a new world. And I've got just the thing—a fine bottle of well-aged Scotch from Earth."

Rachel grinned. "I'd be delighted to join you in a toast," she said as he led her toward the nearest briefing room.

Chapter Five

THE TIME FOR DEPARTURE was already upon them. It was hard for James Kirk to believe that less than a month had passed since the *Hawking* had been discovered.

"Ready, Scotty?" Kirk asked at his bridge command station.

"As ready as we'll ever be, Captain," Scotty's voice replied from the engineering deck.

"Then take us out, Mr. Sulu," Kirk said.

"Aye, aye, sir," the helmsman said from his post in front of Kirk.

The starship moved ahead on impulse power, to test the stability of the tractor beam that held the *Hawking* below the *Enterprise*. Leander Cortés and his people had insisted on staying aboard their ship during this last test, instead of returning to the *Enterprise* temporarily. If the beam held, as they clearly expected it would, they wanted to be on their way to their new home as soon as possible.

"All secure," Spock said from his bridge station aft.

In the warp, all inertial resistances in the attached mass of the *Hawking* would be neutralized; but Kirk wanted to be sure that the tractor beam buttresses would hold even within conventional inertial stresses. He was transporting a valuable antique, he told himself, as well as some precious examples of human history.

"All secure," Spock repeated, "all stresses normal and well within all possible tolerances, as expected." Kirk heard a tone in Spock's voice that suggested that actual testing had been unnecessary after all the parameters had been put into place. A Vulcan's pride in his reasoning was a subtle thing, but Kirk had learned to detect evidence of it in his friend's speech.

"Prepare for warp drive," Kirk said, sitting back.

"Aye, aye, Captain," Chekov said from his navigator's station at Sulu's right.

"Lieutenant Uhura," Kirk said, "open a link to the *Hawking*." The image of Leander Cortés appeared on the viewscreen. "Are you ready, Captain Cortés?"

"Yes," Cortés replied. "It's a big day for us. We're all— I don't quite know how to describe it. To say we're excited, or grateful, or even ecstatic—none of those words seems adequate. This is an event we thought we'd never experience."

Kirk nodded. "I understand."

"And we're all eagerly anticipating our first sight of Merope Four. Even those who were hesitant about settling there at first are now looking forward to a life on a world that seems so strangely . . . familiar."

It was, Kirk realized, a day of liberation for the exiles from Earth. They had fled the horrors of their home world only to find another prison, one that fixed them in a black sky as surely as if a vise had gripped their ship. Once any vessel fell below the slowing of time in relativistic travel, the shortness of energy and human lifespan imposed space-time's interstellar quarantine.

"Ahead, warp one," he said, appreciating anew the ingenuity and thought that had freed humanity to roam among the stars. It was a miracle, by the thinking of past ages, a bending of physical law to human wishes. Kirk thought of the American West, the crossing of which had once taken many months, yet which even in the twentieth century could be crossed in hours. "Bring it up to warp four, Mr. Sulu. We're not going very far."

As the *Enterprise* and the *Hawking* flashed out of warp and entered a standard orbit around Merope IV, the planet's sun brightened the *Enterprise*'s viewscreen. Uhura turned from her console to gaze at the image of the planet.

New Niger, the largest of Merope IV's three continents, the only one in the southern hemisphere, and the only one so far inhabited by human colonists, had a population of about two hundred forty thousand people. Some forty thousand of them lived in New Ibadan, the only community that was even close to the size of a city. The rest inhabited small settlements to the east and west; three of these were near the Temba River, which ran past

New Ibadan. The Temba was a great river, nearly as long as the Nile.

The earliest colonists had been largely from West Africa, although over the years people from various regions of Earth and from other colony worlds had settled on Merope IV. The political arrangements of the colonists, according to Starfleet records, consisted of elected town councils and a city council that governed New Ibadan, all of which were overseen by a leader known as the First Citizen, who was appointed by the members of the various councils. Uhura had learned from the records that only one person had ever held the position of First Citizen, but that was probably because Federation colonists had been on Merope IV for only forty years, and their councils had existed for less than a decade.

Captain Kirk finished his coffee and handed the cup back to Ruchi Padma, the yeoman on duty. "Hailing frequency, Captain?" Uhura asked, expecting an order from the captain. The city council of New Ibadan had sent them a subspace message a week ago, saying that they would welcome the Earthfolk from the *Hawking* as new settlers, but the leader would now be expecting a greeting from Captain Kirk.

"Yes," Kirk said, "it's time for some diplomacy. Contact the office of the First Citizen."

Uhura had already turned back to her console to set up the link. Behind her, she heard the captain say, "This is Captain James T. Kirk of the *U.S.S. Enterprise*, with the *Stephen Hawking* in tow. You are expecting us."

After a few moments of silence, a man's voice replied,

"Welcome, Captain Kirk. The First Citizen has been waiting to speak with you."

Uhura knew that voice well. She had not expected ever to hear that voice again. She turned toward the bridge viewscreen and saw a brown-skinned man with closely cropped black hair and widely set brown eyes. He was older now, and his face had grown more angular, as if age had chiseled away the softer flesh of youth, but otherwise he looked much the same.

Feelings of remorse and regret welled up inside her as she thought of the man with whom she had once expected to spend the rest of her life. She had believed that she had put those feelings behind her long ago.

"I am Trent Aristotle Ojuremi," the man on the viewscreen said, "aide and assistant to our colony's leader and spokesperson, First Citizen Teressa Aliss." His eyes seemed to be peering into the bridge as if it were a small puppet stage and he was anxiously trying to note the figures. "We have been anticipating your arrival ... with, I must confess, much discussion, ever since our message saying that we would welcome the *Hawking*'s passengers was sent to you."

"The people aboard the *Hawking*," Captain Kirk said, "are very much looking forward to being among you."

"The First Citizen is also looking forward to conversing with you, Captain. She is at a meeting of the New Ibadan city council now, but you will be able to speak to her very soon." Trent Ojuremi, Uhura thought, seemed to be staring directly at her, although that had to be an illusion; Trent would be concentrating on the captain and his words. "What I would like to ask now," Ojuremi continued, "is something about the character of the people you are bringing to us. Are any of them criminals?"

"I know of one among them who, you might say, has a less than exemplary record," the captain replied, "but I wouldn't call him a hardened criminal by any means. I remind you that those aboard the *Hawking* come from a time when people sometimes resorted to illegal activities simply in order to survive, or to help those who were dependent on them."

"You needn't fill me in on past history, Captain," Ojuremi said. "We don't mind having resourceful people here, even if some of their past activities may have been shady. But pathological criminals are another matter. Is there any chance any such individuals could be among the *Hawking*'s passengers?"

"Not that we've been able to ascertain," Kirk said, "but the records from that time are fragmentary."

"You will, of course, continue to check on anything you can and keep us informed."

"Naturally, Mr. Ojuremi," the captain said, and Uhura heard the annoyance in Kirk's voice. Trent did not sound as though he was ready to welcome anyone from the *Hawking*. She wondered if he was simply giving vent to his own views, or was reflecting the growing doubts of other Meropeans. Maybe it would not be possible to land Leander Cortés and his people at this colony world after all. Trent's questions might be the first sign of a refusal.

"Captain Kirk," Ojuremi said then, "will you be available for a discussion with Teressa Aliss in about an hour's time?"

"Yes, I will," Kirk said as the screen abruptly went blank. He turned and looked around at the others on the bridge. "Now there's a man in a hurry!"

"He sure didn't sound," Sulu said, "as if he was getting ready to roll out the red carpet."

"Captain," Uhura said, "I know the man."

The captain turned toward her. "Lieutenant?"

"I knew Trent Ojuremi on Earth," she said, and hesitated.

"What can you tell us?"

"I don't know if anything I can tell you is relevant. Trent and I were very close when we were young. We went to the same school during our teens, and we once dreamed of serving in Starfleet together." Uhura averted her eyes for a moment. "Trent failed to win admission to the Academy. He was very unhappy about that, angry and resentful about his failure." She lifted her head. "I lost track of him years ago, but I did hear occasionally from other friends that he was at loose ends and very bitter about the way his life had gone."

"You could leave, Uhura." Trent had said that to her during her second year at Starfleet Academy. He had come there to see her, cornering her outside a classroom, insisting that he had to talk to her. "Leave," he said, "and come away with me." He had wanted her to throw away what he could not have for himself, and she had not been willing to do that. She had never regretted her decision to remain at the Academy, but the pain inside her had persisted for some years afterward, flaring up whenever she thought of Trent.

Captain Kirk was silent for a bit. "Well," he said at

last, "now that he's the assistant to this colony's leader, we may conclude that he's pulled himself together. To come to a new Federation settlement, endure harsher conditions than many on Earth are used to, and rise to a position of some importance is something of an accomplishment."

"That's true," Uhura said, wanting to believe the captain. The Trent Ojuremi she had known had been a gifted student, a young man who could have won admission to any university in Africa, any university on Earth. Any of the young women in their secondary school would have welcomed his attentions; all of the young men had tried to emulate his intellectual and athletic accomplishments. Trent had been one of those blessed youths who glowed with promise, who could have had anything he wanted—except admission to Starfleet Academy. Uhura had been torn between her own joy at being accepted by the Academy and bewilderment at their rejection of Trent. Starfleet Academy rejected many fine applicants; everyone knew that. Only later, after hearing of Trent's aimless and seemingly wasted life, had Uhura begun to suspect that the officers at Starfleet Academy might have seen signs of some flaw in his character when they had made their decision to turn him down.

He might have changed in the years since then. He was on Merope IV, helping to build a new world, obviously trusted by the colony's leaders. He must have changed, Uhura told herself, trying to forget the hostile tone that had come into his voice while he was speaking to Captain Kirk.

* * *

Kirk looked up from the report he had been reading about Teressa Aliss. The First Citizen of Merope IV had been born to two of the earliest settlers. Her education consisted largely of downloaded courses from the Federation's data banks in biology and political science. She had been chosen for the post of First Citizen ten years ago, when she was barely twenty-six.

That particular fact, Kirk thought, was significant. For the Meropeans on the councils to trust such a young person with their highest office meant that she must have done something to earn respect.

"Captain Kirk," Uhura said from her station, "First Citizen Teressa Aliss is hailing us."

"Open a channel," Kirk replied as he looked up at the viewscreen. The Meropean leader was early. As the screen blinked on, he saw a mahogany-skinned woman with short white-blonde hair, hazel eyes, and high, angular cheekbones.

"Greetings, Captain Kirk," Teressa Aliss said in a deep alto voice.

"Greetings, First Citizen," Kirk responded as he got to his feet.

"Captain, please do sit down. Please let us keep the protocol to a minimum. I'll come right to the point. Some Meropeans have grown increasingly concerned about the possible presence of criminals and other undesirables among the people of the *Hawking*. Let me add that, as far as I'm concerned, our agreement to accept the colonists stands. Starfleet transmitted all the information they had to us, and there is probably little else we can find out about them, but still some have doubts."

Kirk waited for her to continue, then said, "Of course you know that the records from those times are incomplete."

"Yes," Teressa Aliss murmured, "and this captain of their ship, this Leander Cortés, may also have lied to you."

"I don't think he would, Ms. Aliss. I've had some time to get to know the man, and he's not a liar. You have my word on that."

"I would certainly never doubt your word, Captain," the First Citizen said. "It is reassuring to hear that you have some trust in Leander Cortés. But I ask that you have a probing discussion with Captain Cortés about this matter, and then report back to me. If nothing disturbing emerges from your discussion, we'll proceed as planned."

"I understand," Kirk said, wishing that this issue had been raised earlier.

"Please realize," the Meropean leader said in what sounded like a more congenial tone, "that we do need more people, as many as we can get. New Niger is still sparsely populated, and there are two other continents to settle. In all honesty, not all of the people who have come here to live have spotless reputations. Colony worlds should be places where people can get a fresh start. We need settlers of all kinds—that was why we were unquestioning in our initial communications. But sometimes people have second thoughts after reflection."

"I do understand." Kirk maintained his composure.

"I know you do. These early years of our colony will

set the example for our future. I hope to make that future as good as it can be, as much as it is in our power to do so."

Kirk could see the resolve in Teressa Aliss's face. "Very well," he said, "I'll speak with Captain Cortés."

"We have enough problems at the moment," she added, "without creating new ones. We do need more colonists, but not new problems." She narrowed her eyes slightly, and Kirk knew that she was going to press her point as far as it was necessary to learn what she needed to know. "Captain, tell me truthfully, what is your opinion of these people you have brought to us? You are a Starfleet officer with an excellent reputation—you see, I looked at your record, too." She paused, as if waiting to see if she might have offended him. "I know I can trust your judgment, so what do you think?"

"Truthfully," Kirk said, "I think it's wise to proceed with caution. Captain Cortés and his people have done their best to behave cooperatively and constructively, but they have also survived a lengthy ordeal. Psychologically, they're still recovering from that. But I have every reason to think that the arrival of these people will be productive for your colony. I would expect some minor problems, but nothing serious."

"Minor problems are one thing. We don't need more serious ones."

Kirk thought of what the woman had implied earlier. "You mentioned other problems," he said. "Of what sort are they?"

Her eyes shifted; she looked distinctly uneasy. At last she said, "I would like to discuss that with you in person, after I hear more from you about the character of those aboard the *Hawking*."

"I'll look forward to our meeting," Kirk said.

"As will I, Captain Kirk." The First Citizen's image vanished.

Kirk remained at his station, thinking. He knew about Dmitri Glakov, Chekov's relative, but now wondered if he would have found out even that much without Chekov's knowledge of his family history. Even so, he and Chekov had to take Glakov's word that his criminal exploits had been greatly exaggerated. Now he was wondering how many others among Cortés's companions might have things to hide. There would be little in any records to contradict any stories they chose to tell.

"Lieutenant Uhura." Kirk stood up. "Contact Captain Cortés and ask him to prepare to be beamed aboard. Tell him that I have to meet with him immediately."

Kirk had put the matter as delicately as he could, but saw from the expression on Leander Cortés's face that the other man was dismayed by the situation. The Meropeans had said that they would accept these new settlers, and now some were already having doubts about that decision.

"Well," Cortés muttered as he sat back in his chair, "I don't particularly care for the idea of going where we're not wanted."

"That isn't quite accurate," Kirk said. "The First Citizen is willing to abide by the agreement, and she hasn't indicated that the concerns about your people are widespread."

"You needn't gloss it over, Captain. It would be hard enough for us to settle there even if the Meropeans were unanimous in welcoming us."

"I have to ask you this," Kirk said, "and I know you'll be honest with me. Are there any outright criminals among your shipmates whom we haven't been told about?"

Cortés gazed at him steadily. "You realize," the older man said, "that I would have to know the people aboard our ship pretty damned well by now, that if I hadn't known everything about all of them at the start, I would certainly have found out what kind of people they were later on."

Kirk nodded.

"I have to tell you that there are some whom you would call dubious characters," he went on. "You already know about Dmitri Glakov. Laure Vidor was a thief as a girl, largely because there weren't too many other ways for her to feed herself. Anthony Tikriti sold the security codes of residential buildings to burglars—he had a gift for hacking into the computers that controlled them. Xavier Rodriguez dealt in illegal pharmaceuticals in order to help his dying son, not that he was able to save the boy in the end. I could tell you other such stories, even make you a list if you like. By your clearly more civilized standards, some of my comrades might be classed as scoundrels, at the very least. Not all of them. But some."

"You don't seem very concerned about the . . . questionable ones," Kirk said.

"I'm not."

"Yet you didn't say anything about them earlier."

Cortés stood up and paced on the other side of the table, then stopped again behind his chair. "Captain Kirk, these people have been locked up in the equivalent of a prison for decades. They have gotten to know one another as few people ever do. Whatever they were in the past, whatever crimes they committed—that's all been wrung out of them as surely as if they had been bled—the bad and, I fear, maybe some of the good." He sighed. "But now they're looking to a better life again. I, along with you and your crew, have been trying to draw them out, and in a climate of fear, I worry they may turn inward again."

"The people you've mentioned," Kirk said, "don't sound as if they were violent or pathological criminals."

"None of them were. Whatever criminal tendencies they had were directed mostly to stealing or other kinds of larceny, but what would there be to steal, what has there been to steal during our voyage? Every one of them stood up under pressure, every one of them put the welfare of others ahead of his own. Are any of them less than admirable because of what they did long ago? Can I guarantee that they will not become violent or commit other crimes under any circumstances? Maybe not. But can you ensure that among your crew not a single one will ever go wrong?"

Kirk shook his head, remembering the misguided actions of his former officer Marla McGivers. "Of course not."

"What are they asking of us down there?" Cortés

asked, "that we pass some kind of test to be allowed into their shining colony?"

"No, that isn't what's going on here," Kirk replied. "They're merely being cautious. Teressa Aliss, their leader, has said that she's willing to abide by her world's promise to Starfleet. They need new people, as many as they can get. After a while, your people will have other choices—whether to stay, go on to other colonies, maybe even return to Earth."

Cortés sat down again. "I think my people, most of them, will elect to stay together."

"That may change in time," Kirk said.

"Captain, I can see where you might feel justified in feeling that I misled you. But I didn't bring up this business of criminal records earlier because I considered it a dead issue. What is more important about Xavier Rodriguez, that he once dealt in illegal medical drugs or that he used his medical knowledge to save some lives aboard the *Hawking?* Does it matter more that Anthony Tikriti once used his mathematical talents to crack security codes, or that he was able to nurse our old computers along and reprogram them when some of us feared they might fail? All the fight has been taken out of us. A colony will give us a new start."

Kirk nodded, feeling sympathy for the man. "I can well understand that you thought the issue would never come up again. I'd also bet that not all the people of Merope Four are angels."

"I think we all realized, once we were on our way to this colony, that the truth would come out eventually." Cortés rested his hands on the table. "But there's a big difference between finding out, after you've been around someone for a while and come to know him and trust him, that he was once a thief, and knowing about his past before you even have a chance to get acquainted with him. He's tainted in your mind right from the start. He doesn't get as much of a chance."

"I see your point," Kirk said. "I've seen how you've handled yourself since we found your ship. I told Teressa Aliss that you and your people have behaved very well."

Cortés sank back in his chair, looking relieved. "Maybe it would be better if we were set down as far from this colony as possible, and permitted to start our own. This planet has three continents, two of which are still unsettled. I don't see how we could be of any concern to the Meropeans if we were that far away from their settlements."

"My feeling," Kirk said, "and it's backed up by Dr. McCoy and his medical team, is that both your people and the Meropeans will benefit more from closer ties, at least at first. You'll need their help and advice in the beginning, and that will help you put the horrors of your long voyage behind you. There won't be anything to stop you or any other group from setting out on your own one day. A planet is a big place."

Cortés managed a faint smile. "As well we know, in memory." He sat up again. "I am willing to do the following. I can give you the records of everyone on board the *Hawking*, for you to pass along to this Meropean leader and any governing body. If she's a reasonable sort, she'll see after she's read them that she has little to fear from us. If we are going to live among these people, I suppose we must try to show some trust in their judgment."

"I'll do better than that," Kirk said. "I'll also send two of my officers down there to go over the records with the First Citizen, and answer any other questions she may have." That was not his only reason for seizing a chance to send two emissaries. He thought of how uneasy Teressa Aliss had looked when he had asked her about the problems of her colony. It would be useful to have the impressions of two of his people and their assessment of the leader. "All of that," he continued, "should do a lot to reassure her."

"I hope so, and I hope that's all that's needed. It would be ironic if, after having come so far both in space and in time, we found that we couldn't escape from our pasts after all."

Kirk wondered if that would be enough. What, he thought, is Cortés never going to tell me? Given what he has told me already, if there is anything else, is it still better off being buried? Maybe so; being distrusted from the start might even provoke some of his shipmates to behave badly, to feel that they would never be accepted.

As Kirk looked at this captain from the past, he realized that this man was also looking forward to passing the torch to new leaders, that he was tired of pointing the way, of holding hearts and minds together for so long. But he still understood that he could not let go irresponsibly, that in his small sample of humanity there was no one to replace him easily; it would take new circumstances to shape new leaders and bring new visions.

"Captain Cortés," Kirk said, "let me assure you that the *Enterprise* will stay here as long as it takes to settle your people properly and to mediate where necessary."

"I'm grateful for that," Cortés replied, "and for everything else you've done. I only hope that the people waiting to receive us will be as reasonable and as understanding of us as you have been."

Chapter Six

TERESSA ALISS finally lifted her eyes from the small viewscreen in front of her and looked across her desk at Uhura. "Lieutenant," the First Citizen murmured, "these records do ease most of my doubts about the *Hawking*'s passengers. What you have told me about your own encounters with them has also been helpful."

Uhura sat with Farley Longstreet on one of the benches facing Teressa Aliss's desk. "Captain Kirk will be most gratified to hear that," Uhura said. "They're all good people, First Citizen. They'll be assets to your colony."

The Meropean leader leaned back and rested her hands on the arms of her carved wooden chair. "I'll recommend to our other councils that we welcome these new settlers as soon as possible."

Uhura glanced at Longstreet. Teressa Aliss had greeted

them cordially, offering them beverages made from indigenous fruits and a tray of tiny pastries while she perused the records the *Enterprise* had sent to her. The First Citizen's questions had been intelligent and pointed, and Uhura could report to the captain that her impression of Aliss was favorable.

Yet the Meropean woman had seemed distracted from time to time. A message had come in earlier, something about an outlying settlement—Uhura had not been able to hear more than a few words from across the room— and Aliss had frowned at her desk viewscreen before abruptly cutting the call short. Every so often, even in the middle of a sentence, she had looked toward her small screen as if expecting to get a message that might contain bad news.

Aliss stood up. "I've been at this desk all day," she said. "Let me invite you to take a short walk on the plaza with me before you beam back to your ship."

Uhura and Longstreet got to their feet. "We'll gladly accept your offer," Longstreet replied. "We'd like to see some more of New Ibadan."

Aliss led them across the room. A long window with glass doors faced a wide plaza paved with flat polished blue flagstones. The First Citizen slid one of the doors open and led them outside.

Uhura breathed in some of the crisp, cool air. The plaza was bounded by small wooden buildings of no more than one or two stories each, most of which looked like residences. The building that housed the First Citizen's office, at four stories, was the tallest structure Uhura could see. To the east, a wide staircase led up to what looked like a large terrace. Near every building were small gardens of brightly colored flowers.

A bird that resembled a falcon swooped toward the terrace. Other people were out on the plaza, taking strolls or sitting on benches outside the nearby buildings to talk, most of them clothed in ankle-length caftans or colorful tunics and pants. Several men and women nodded at Teressa Aliss as she passed or touched their hands to their foreheads in greeting.

"Over there is the Alim al-Reyhan Primary School," Aliss said, gesturing at a one-story building with large windows where a group of children had gathered outside. "It's the third school for young children we've built in New Ibadan, and we'll soon need another. We still don't have a university, I'm afraid, but we're on our way to starting one."

Uhura glimpsed a man in the distance who resembled Trent Ojuremi, then realized her mistake. Part of her had been hoping to see him again; part of her had been dreading the prospect. Trent had not been in Teressa Aliss's office when she and Longstreet had beamed down, and had not come there at all to greet them. That might mean nothing except that he had other more pressing duties. It might also mean that he was deliberately avoiding her.

A dark-haired woman in a scarlet robe waved at them from across the plaza, then hurried toward them. "Teressa," the woman called out as she approached, "have you heard anything about what's going on at—"

Aliss jerked her head toward Uhura and Longstreet. The other woman halted and stared at Uhura's uniform as

69

if she had just recognized the lieutenant's Starfleet insignia. "Oh," she said, "excuse me. I didn't mean to interrupt anything."

"Lieutenants Uhura and Longstreet of the *Enterprise*," Aliss said smoothly. "They have beamed down to discuss the new settlers who will most likely soon be joining our community."

The dark-haired woman nodded her head in their direction, and Uhura saw a look of fear in her eyes. Something was worrying her, and Uhura was certain that it was not just the presence of Starfleet or the arrival of new settlers.

"And I haven't heard anything more," the First Citizen continued, "so you needn't worry. Rumors have a way of making things seem worse than they are, and there's no point in worrying until there's no alternative."

"I suppose so," the other woman said, looking doubtful.

Aliss turned toward Uhura. "I wish that I could spend more time with you both," she said, "but I'm neglecting some of my other obligations."

In other words, Uhura thought, it's time for us to go. "Captain Kirk will look forward to meeting with you himself soon," Uhura said.

Longstreet took out his communicator and flipped it open. "Longstreet here," he said. "Two to beam up."

She struggled, knowing that she was caught in a dream but unable to wake herself. Parts of her memory were already gone—most of her childhood, scraps of subjects and skills that she had worked hard to master. The humid green warmth was all around her now, pressing in on her, threatening to engulf her completely.

"No," she cried out, and the word tore itself from her throat.

Teressa Aliss was awake. She lay in bed, thinking of how hard it had been to get out of her dream this time. The dream—it was the same dream she had dreamed last night and the night before that. She had dreamed it as a child, waking herself and her parents with her screams.

After the third time, she had told her mother about what she had dreamed.

"I have the same dream," Teressa's mother had told her. "Your father dreams it, too. But it doesn't come to us very often, and it's only a dream, so you mustn't be afraid."

Not long after that, while still a child, Teressa had learned that many of the people in New Ibadan had dreamed her dream. Most of them had dreamed it only once or twice; others had never dreamed it at all. That so many people had dreamed exactly the same dream was a remarkable coincidence, and would have been worth investigating if the dreams had persisted, but soon no one was dreaming that dream any more. The dream that had troubled so many Meropeans in the past had become a forgotten curiosity until a couple of weeks ago, when one of Teressa's neighbors had told her of a nightmare that had troubled her.

Others in the city had dreamed the dream since then. Teressa had made some discreet inquiries of physicians and teachers and parents of small children, and had discovered that, during the past week, at least one hundred of New Ibadan's residents had dreamed of the warmth and the green and of losing parts of themselves and their memories. By then, the dream was coming to Teressa every night, and each time it seemed harder for her to wake from it.

Now, as she got up and crossed the room to her desk, she thought of the settlement near Shaku, and the fact that people had begun to have their nightmares just before that settlement had been wiped out.

Teressa shook herself. That had to be chance, she told herself, wanting to believe it. She was not one to believe that dreams were harbingers or warnings; that was magical thinking, and she prided herself on being a realist.

She sat down at her desk. She had reviewed all of the records that Captain James T. Kirk had transmitted about the people aboard the *Hawking*. There was no one among them who truly worried her, and Captain Kirk's two lieutenants had assured her that all of them were looking forward to the new life that awaited them. Even if Leander Cortés had shaded the truth a little—and given Captain Kirk's assessment of the man and his own experience with him, along with the testimony of Uhura and Longstreet, she doubted that Cortés was an outright liar—the *Hawking*'s passengers were older people worn down by their long ordeal, grateful to have come to the end of their long journey.

Older, she reminded herself, by their standards, anyway. Captain Kirk had pointed that out in the report he had attached to the *Hawking*'s documents. These people, thanks to the efforts of the *Enterprise*'s medical personnel, might seem as if they were in their prime, and physiologically they were, but by the standards of their time they were well into middle age or close to being elderly. They were unlikely to engage in much criminal enterprise here; Lieutenant Longstreet had emphasized that even the violent criminals of their time, as a general rule, had tended to be young rather than old. There was no real reason to turn these people away, and she had said so in her report to the city and town councils. As it was, given the incident at the new settlement near Shaku, her world might soon have need of people with the fortitude that Cortés's voyagers had shown during their journey.

Teressa got up and walked toward the window at the other end of the room. Her living quarters were three floors up in the four-story building that housed the New Ibadan City Council offices, meeting rooms, and apartments of the council members and their families. The City Council building was the tallest in the city; her window overlooked the wide expanse of the Yakuru Plaza. She gazed out at the small houses nestled among the trees on the other side of the plaza, at the pathway that led from the newly built Alim al-Reyhan Primary School down to the bank of the Temba River, and the sight of all that greenery—all that life—suddenly frightened her.

Trent Ojuremi was waiting for Teressa in her office when she entered, sitting on one of the benches that faced her desk. "Better close the door," he said. It was an atypical request; usually she left her door open in the mornings, the time set aside for any Meropeans who wished to meet with her.

Teressa slid the door shut. Trent rested his back against the wall behind him. "The rescue team has returned to Shaku," he continued. "They found a boy near the site. There's nothing left, Teressa. One hundred and seven people are gone, the whole community is gone. That boy was the only survivor."

She went to her desk and sat down in her chair. The first distress call from the new settlement north of Shaku had come in only two days ago, saying that fissures were forming around the town. By the time a rescue team had been sent out from Shaku, a second report had told of a wall of moss growing out from the fissures.

"What happened?" she asked.

"The boy said that the moss . . . engulfed the settlement, simply swallowed it up, people and houses and all. He had wandered away from the settlement before the fissures first appeared—he'd had some sort of argument with his father and had gone storming out of the house. When he went back, the fissures had opened too wide for him to leap across them. He was cut off—he couldn't get near the place. All he could do was watch from a hill while the whole community was swallowed up, engulfed by a wall of matted moss."

"Maybe we'd better think of evacuating Shaku," Teressa said.

"I suggested that to Messanga Watson and the rest of the Shaku town council. He says that most of the people are willing to remain there, although a few families are sending their children to stay with relatives here in New Ibadan. If Messanga notices anything strange—"

"If he does," she said, "I hope he'll have time to get those people to safety." Losing one hundred and seven people was bad enough. Over a thousand lived in Shaku.

"Messanga's older daughter was one of the people who was lost," Trent said, "along with his grandson. He's dealing with that, too."

"I am sorry to hear that."

"What are we going to do about those Earthfolk that Starfleet wants us to accept as settlers?" Trent asked.

Teressa glanced at her aide and caught a glint of anger in his dark eyes. He had asked to be excused from her meeting with Longstreet and Uhura; Trent clearly did not care for the necessity of dealing with Captain Kirk of the *Enterprise* or any other representative of Starfleet.

"We have some time," she replied. "The other councils have only just received my report and my recommendation that we welcome those people."

"They'll go along with you, Teressa. They always have."

"I expect that they will, but we'll still have to decide where the new arrivals are going to be settled. By then, we ought to know more about what happened near Shaku, and then—"

"I'm worried, Teressa," Trent interrupted. "That land was surveyed before those people settled there. Fissures opening up, mats of moss engulfing towns—there was no indication that the ground there was so unstable, that anything like this could happen."

Teressa gazed at him without speaking. Her aide was a gifted man, probably a brilliant one. He had come to Merope IV with degrees from two of Earth's finest universities, and she had overlooked the fact that some years of his youth were unaccounted for in his personal record. Thanks to Trent Ojuremi, who had drawn up the plans and found ten other people willing to join him as faculty members, they now had the beginnings of an institution of higher learning in New Ibadan. Teressa, only too aware of her own sketchy education, made it a point to attend Trent's lectures in physics, and had learned much from him. But occasionally she glimpsed a part of him that seemed hidden—a touchiness, a lack of decisiveness, too great a willingness to take offense where none was intended. She benefited from his advice, while recognizing that he might not have made a good leader or council member himself.

Still, Trent, whatever his faults, had contributed much to the life of Merope IV. She had considered that while pondering the records of Leander Cortés and his people, who might also benefit her world. Yet another reason for accepting those new settlers was Captain Kirk's recommendation that she do so. The captain was clearly an intelligent and perceptive Starfleet officer, with a superior record and several decorations to his credit. That his judgment of Leander Cortés was probably correct was demonstrated by Cortés's willingness to reveal some less than admirable facts about his companions that he could easily have concealed.

"I'll tell Messanga Watson to keep an eye on things around Shaku," Teressa murmured, "and to inform us immediately if he notices anything out of the ordinary. In the meantime, we should proceed with plans for settling Leander Cortés and his people once I hear from all of the councils."

"I suppose you're right," Trent said, sounding as though he still had doubts. "Starfleet, of course, always knows best." There was a harshness in his voice that she had not heard before. "There's one thing I forgot to mention about that lost settlement."

"Yes?"

"The survivor—that boy—told Messanga about a dream several people in his settlement were having some days before the fissures first appeared. What's odd is that these people were having the same dream, of being engulfed, of forgetting parts of their lives. I don't know what it can mean, but—"

Teressa waved a hand at him, motioning to him to be silent. "I have had those dreams, Trent," she said. "I had them when I was a child. Other people had them, too, my parents had them, and then they went away. And now, just over the past few days, I've begun to have those dreams again."

"Did anything unusual happen after you started dreaming those dreams, back when you were first having them?" Trent asked.

She shook her head. "No, and after a while, they went away, as I said."

"Then that's probably what will happen this time. It's coincidence, that's all."

Trent did not fool her. He was trying to convince both of them that there was nothing to the dreaming, but he knew as well as she did that on any alien world, even on a planet as Earthlike as this one, a world that had been carefully surveyed by Starfleet before settlement and that humans had been living on for some time, nothing could be taken for granted.

"You'll be pleased to know," Teressa Aliss said from the viewscreen, "that all of our councils have voted to welcome the people of the *Hawking*. We also have more than enough families in New Ibadan who are willing to open their homes to the new settlers until they decide where they want to live permanently."

Kirk smiled, trying to ignore his apprehensions. Uhura and Longstreet had reported to him that the First Citizen seemed to be wrestling with a problem of some kind involving her colony.

"Good," Kirk said, "and I'm sure that Captain Cortés will be equally happy to know that he and his people officially have a new home." The plan was to disperse the new colonists among various Meropean homes in New Ibadan; from there, they could eventually filter out individually or in small groups to the smaller outlying towns, remain in the city, or gather together again to start their own community.

Both Kirk and Cortés had agreed, when Teressa Aliss had first suggested it, that the initial dispersal might be a welcome break from the enforced togetherness of the long voyage aboard the *Hawking*. Couples and close friends would be settled in the same households, so as to lessen any shock of being suddenly isolated from comrades. Yet Kirk still wondered whether the Meropean woman wanted to disperse the new settlers out of a lingering distrust.

"I hope that we can start beaming people down soon," Kirk continued. "They're all anxious to see sunlight again, and breathe some fresh air."

The First Citizen's smile faded. "We still need some more time to . . . make arrangements," she murmured. "But that shouldn't take more than another couple of days. What we'd like to do is to have a reception for the new settlers, in order to welcome them here and introduce them to the people who are taking them into their homes. Naturally, you and your crew are also invited to attend—you could probably use the shore leave."

"We'd be delighted to accept," Kirk said.

"I also have another request," the Meropean woman said. "I would like to meet personally with Leander Cortés as soon as possible, here in my office. A personal meeting between us is advisable. I should know if any of his people need any special attention, or might be better off in a particular home rather than another, and he should also visit the city where they will be living for a while."

"I understand," Kirk said. "I'll speak to Captain Cortés immediately, and arrange to beam him down." He thought of what Uhura and Longstreet had told him. "Perhaps I should also come along with him, so that we can all meet together."

The First Citizen's eyes shifted slightly. "I would

rather meet him alone first. That might make him feel that we are truly ready to welcome him and his shipmates, rather than accepting them only out of some obligation to Starfleet."

"I see your point." That request might be a sign of Teressa Aliss's sensitivity; it might also be another sign that she was indeed trying to hide something that she was not yet ready to reveal. Cortés and his people had a right to know what hidden difficulties they might face on Merope IV, but Kirk also did not want to provoke the Meropean leader into a confrontation that might end in her rejecting the new settlers after all.

Leander Cortés and his comrades, Kirk thought, had been through enough without having to endure that.

"I am pleased that you understand," Teressa Aliss said.

"But I still would prefer to have someone with him," Kirk said, "if only because this will be the first time Leander Cortés has ever set foot on any planet except Earth. That might be disorienting for him. It wouldn't hurt for him to have a familiar person nearby." He wanted one of his officers there to assess the situation.

The woman lifted her head; her face grew more taut, and Kirk had the impression that she had suddenly made a decision. "Yes, of course," she said. "I didn't think of that."

"I'd like to send my chief medical officer along with him," Kirk said. "Captain Cortés and his people have spent more time with my medical personnel than with almost anyone else on my ship, and Dr. McCoy will also be able to reassure you about how well they're doing."

"Very well, Captain Kirk."

The First Citizen had taken McCoy and Cortés for a walk along the Temba River waterfront, then led the two men to an open-air cafe where they were served an herb tea that tasted of mint while Teressa Aliss made entries on a portable screen about which of the new settlers might need special consideration. She had assured the captain of the *Hawking* that there were more than enough families to welcome them into their homes, and others willing to accept them when it was time for a change.

McCoy offered his own recommendations—this person showed signs of agoraphobia after long confinement on the *Hawking,* that person might do better in a home with people who would draw her out of her darker moods—and all the while, he had the feeling that Teressa Aliss was holding something back from them.

He looked out at the river. On the southern bank, across from the city of New Ibadan, was a flat green plain and patches of blue wildflowers. Small red birds darted among the flowers, alighting from time to time on the wide blue petals. This was a beautiful world, with room to grow. The people from the *Hawking,* McCoy knew, could be content here. He did not want to think that the seeming paradise of Merope IV might be harboring a serpent.

"I think that about does it," Cortés said to Teressa

Aliss. "As for the rest of us, most of us are adaptable souls. We won't need any pampering."

"To have endured the voyage you did—" The Meropean paused. "It says a lot for you and your companions, Captain Cortés."

"Perhaps it was worth it to reach such a place as this. The trees in your city, the green, the birds—it's been a long time since I've seen so much green, so much life."

"I wish I could tell you that you have nothing to worry about here," the First Citizen said, "apart from the usual problems of adjusting to a new life in a young colony." She glanced at McCoy with her lovely hazel eyes. "But that isn't the case, I'm afraid. You've been through an ordeal already. You don't need to be surprised later on by a new problem that's worrying us now."

Cortés sat back in his chair. Here it comes, McCoy thought, the thing she's been trying to hide.

Teressa Aliss drank some tea, then set her cup down. "We had an incident in one of our northern settlements . . . a disaster, and one we don't understand. A community of one hundred and seven people was simply swallowed up by the ground. There was only one survivor, a boy, and he described some very strange things."

McCoy drew in his breath sharply; Cortés tensed.

"There wasn't a quake in that region," Teressa Aliss continued, "and we know that the settlement wasn't built on unstable land, over sinkholes or caverns with weakened walls." She went on to talk of what had been reported to her. Fissures had opened up around the town; a green moss-like growth had engulfed the houses and other buildings. The entire settlement had simply disappeared into the ground.

Cortés was silent after the First Citizen finished her story. "I don't suppose," McCoy said at last, "that this is a ploy to scare the captain here and his people away from settling in your colony."

The woman shook her head. "Absolutely not, Dr. McCoy. Maybe it's just one isolated disaster. Maybe it means nothing. But I'd feel a lot better if I knew the cause." She turned to Cortés. "And it isn't fair to let your people come here without telling them that we have this kind of mystery on our hands."

"Do you have anyone investigating the incident?" McCoy asked.

"A rescue team went there from Shaku, the nearest settlement, and returned with the lone survivor. I have their report. No one has gone back to the site of the disaster since then, but that was only a couple of days ago. To be honest, I think they're afraid to go back."

"First Citizen Aliss," McCoy said, "I recommend that you send that report to the *Enterprise* immediately. We might be able to help solve this riddle."

"And what about your people?" she said to Cortés.

"I'll tell them what you have told me," the older man replied. "But I can already guess at what they'll say. They'll want to go ahead with your reception as planned and get themselves settled here. As you say, this may be an isolated incident, in which case there's no reason to panic, and if it isn't—well, we'll sort all that out when the time comes. You've offered us a new home. What kinds of settlers would we show ourselves to be if we turned tail and ran at the first sign of difficulty?"

Leander Cortés, McCoy thought, was showing a lot of strength for a man so recently trapped in a hopeless and desperate situation. Much as he would have liked to take much of the credit for his patient's restored vigor and fortitude, the man's character had been formed long before McCoy had treated him.

"Don't worry, Captain," McCoy said. "We have orders from Starfleet to get you settled before leaving orbit." He smiled at Teressa Aliss. "And we won't leave before we get to the bottom of this disappearance, either."

He sounded very reassuring, even to himself. But his instincts were telling him to be wary.

Chapter Seven

JAMES KIRK materialized on a terrace overlooking the city of New Ibadan. To the west, at the bottom of the steps and gently sloped ramps that led down from the terrace, was a wide plaza; to the south, the Temba River flowed past the city. From here, he could see that most of the buildings in New Ibadan were small square wooden structures with tiled roofs, usually built around courtyards and carefully tended gardens.

He might have been in a small city somewhere in the Pacific Northwest of North America. No, not quite, he thought; the air was cool, but the profusion of brightly colored flowers and leafy fern-like plants reminded him of more tropical climes.

Leander Cortés and Commander Spock had beamed down with him. Spock gazed at the view impassively; Cortés took a deep breath, then sighed.

"We should be happy here," he said.

"Yes, I think you will be," Kirk said, hoping he was right. Teressa Aliss had sent him a brief but disturbing message only a few hours ago.

"I have to talk to you soon, Captain Kirk," she had said. "I'm afraid we do have an additional problem. I hope it's not serious, but I may need your help, and Starfleet's. We'll hold the reception as planned, but I must speak to you there."

He watched as a group of five people from the *Hawking,* Emo Tannan among them, beamed down to where three couples and seven children of varying ages waited. The three families, like the others standing in small groups at various points on the terrace, were people who had offered to take some of the Earthfolk into their homes. A table near Kirk held bowls of fruits and plates of meats and vegetables. Other tables had been set out around the terrace, with what looked like enough food and drink for the entire crew of the *Enterprise* and all of the people from the *Hawking* to have seconds and thirds.

Four more people from the *Hawking* shimmered in near another knot of Meropean families, and were quickly surrounded by people wanting to meet them. They bowed to one another, clasped or shook hands, then stepped aside in twos and threes to converse. Young people carrying trays of food and glasses of colorful beverages moved among the groups, offering refreshments. One blond young man stopped next to Kirk, who took a glass from the tray.

"That's a white wine made from a grape-like fruit indigenous to this planet," the young man said to him.

Kirk took a sip. "Very good," he told the Meropean.

"Reminds me of a superior white Bordeaux."

Cortés and Spock accepted glasses; the young man drifted away. Cortés moved closer to Kirk. "They're making a fine thing of this welcome."

"Indeed they are," Kirk said. Teressa Aliss had still not appeared. He glanced toward the steps leading down to the plaza, looking for her, and saw Trent Ojuremi climbing toward him with a small, brown-haired woman.

"Captain Kirk," Ojuremi said as Kirk stepped toward him, "welcome to Merope Four." The man did not sound at all pleased to see him. "Allow me to introduce you to Dawn Voth, a member of the New Ibadan city council." He gestured at the small woman near him.

"How do you do," Kirk said, then introduced Spock and Leander Cortés to the woman. "Has the First Citizen arrived yet?" he went on.

Ojuremi shook his head. "She'll be here soon."

Kirk was about to mention Teressa Aliss's earlier message, then hesitated. Either her aide already knew that she had sent one, or perhaps she had her own reasons for not wanting him to know about it.

"You will excuse me, Captain Kirk," Ojuremi said. "There are several people here who have claims on my attention."

"Of course, Mr. Ojuremi."

The man was hurrying away almost before the words had left Kirk's mouth.

Pavel Chekov stood with his kinsman Dmitri Glakov on the edge of a knot of people. The two had beamed down with Mr. Scott and Rachel Zlatopolsky, who carried a large shoulder bag filled with personal possessions. A tall, gray-haired Meropean man and a silver-haired woman approached Chekov and the two engineers.

"Rachel Zlatopolsky?" the gray-haired man asked.

"Here she is." Scotty took Rachel's arm and stepped toward the couple. "Allow me to introduce the lass."

"And we're also looking for a Dmitri Glakov," the woman said.

"Greetings." Glakov stepped forward and bowed from the waist. "I am Dmitri Sergeievich Glakov, and this world looks even more beautiful than I had anticipated."

"You both look somewhat younger than the images we saw," the man said. "Wasn't sure I had the right people." He thrust out a hand. "My name's Isaiah Ritchard, and this is my wife, Geraldine Tinko, and we're both mighty pleased to welcome you to New Ibadan."

"I am delighted to meet you," Glakov said as he clasped the Meropean man's hand, then bowed again to the woman, took her hand, and touched his lips to her fingers.

"Hope the both of you don't mind having small children around," Isaiah Ritchard said, "because my daughter and her husband and their three young ones live in the house just across the courtyard from ours."

Rachel smiled. "I love children."

"And so do I," Glakov added. "We have been on a long voyage for too many years without the presence of children. There were times when I wondered if I would ever see a child again."

Chekov looked from the smiling faces of the Meropeans to his kinsman, then caught Scotty's eye. Everything was going very well; he was almost sorry not to be able to spend more time here himself.

Uhura was standing near Christine Chapel and two of the people from the *Hawking* when she saw Trent Ojuremi walking toward her. He wore a long blue shirt made of a fabric that looked like cotton, and loose black pants; he was alone. As he approached, she suddenly felt nervous, wondering if he would still recognize the girl he once had known in her.

"Uhura," he said as he approached, "it has been a long time."

"Yes, it has," she replied.

He bowed slightly in greeting; she inclined her head to him. "You haven't changed at all," he said. "You look almost as I see you in memory. I never expected to see you again, and here you are."

Uhura quickly introduced Christine Chapel and the two Earthpeople with them. Christine smiled, glanced from Uhura to Trent, then excused herself and led the two people from the *Hawking* toward a nearby table.

"You look well, Trent," Uhura murmured, feeling awkward.

"Thank you for saying so. I've had a lot on my mind of late, and feared that might show in my appearance."

She looked away from him for a moment. "You came to a beautiful world," she said, "and the First Citizen obviously values your counsel."

"Teressa may listen to my advice, but she doesn't always take it. I have had some worries about these new colonists."

"You needn't worry about them," Uhura said. "Considering what they've been through, I think they're doing quite well. If anything, they're likely to go out of their way to prove themselves to you."

"After seeing their records, and learning something about the hardships they endured, I don't doubt that. But I was wondering why Starfleet seemed so anxious to have them settle here."

Uhura said, "There were a lot of good reasons—"

"Starfleet and the Federation Council always have their reasons for everything they do. They're so ready to decide others' lives for them." His eyes narrowed. "But of course you would defend Starfleet. It must mean so much to you, being a Starfleet officer, being one of the elect."

It once meant as much to you, Uhura thought. "You know how much it meant to me," she said, "but don't think that the choice I made was easy."

"And have you ever regretted that choice, Uhura?"

She gazed at him steadily. "No."

"Well." His mouth tightened. "I suppose that puts me in my proper place."

"Trent, I didn't come here to spar with you. I've missed you more than you know. I still think of all those times we'd be up late talking about the meaning of life and all the worlds we might see until my mother told you it was time to go home." She put a hand on his arm. For a moment, she thought that he might pull away, but then he covered her hand with his.

Dawn Voth had quickly discovered that she and Leander Cortés shared an interest in ornithology. Kirk, standing to one side with Spock, listened as she spoke of various Meropean bird species.

"Believe it or not," the city councilwoman continued, "we also have a lovely species of waterfowl practically indistinguishable from Earth's trumpeter swans. In fact, the first settlers rather facetiously named them oboe swans, since they make a sound that's a lot like that particular musical instrument."

"I'll be able to get in plenty of birdwatching then," Cortés said.

"Oh, definitely. And our songbirds—not only do they trill delightfully, but they are also quite beautiful. There's one, the Kainji nightingale, that inhabits the Kainji Mountains—that's the range of high mountains in the eastern part of New Niger. Not only does it have a song just like an Earth nightingale's, it also has absolutely gorgeous blue and green plumage."

"Fascinating," Spock murmured.

Dawn Voth peered around Kirk at the steps behind him. "And here comes Teressa now." She took Cortés's arm. "Captain Kirk and Commander Spock, please excuse us. I know Teressa will want to talk to you about various arrangements for the new arrivals, and I'm sure that Captain Cortés would enjoy seeing some of our city birds. A few families of tawny peregrines are nesting in some of the trees bordering the plaza, and we can get a good look at them from the terrace." As she led Cortés away, Kirk had the feeling that the councilwoman already knew what the First Citizen was going to tell him and did not want Cortés to hear it.

He turned to see Teressa Aliss climbing toward him on

Pamela Sargent & George Zebrowski

the steps. She was alone; she wore a long green robe embroidered with gold thread and a matching turban over her hair. She was smaller than he had expected her to be, but her erect posture lent her authority. Her image had shown her to be a beautiful woman; in person, her beauty almost took his breath away.

"Spock," Kirk said, "perhaps you can circulate a bit and see how some of Cortés's people are getting along while I find out what the First Citizen wants to tell me."

"Of course." Spock lifted a brow. "She is a most impressive woman, Captain."

"Believe it or not, that isn't the only thing on my mind. She implied in that last message to me that she wanted to speak to me alone. Let's just hope that, whatever this problem is, it's something easily solved." But he had already noticed the worried look on the face of Teressa Aliss.

The terrace had grown more crowded. Kirk strolled from one group to another with Teressa as she greeted people. She seemed to know almost everyone, addressing each person by name.

"Do you approve?" she asked him after they left one family. "I thought this would be the best way to greet our new settlers, and make them feel welcome, although—" She glanced up at him from the sides of her eyes. "I hope they haven't left one set of hardships behind only to have to deal with another."

"They weren't expecting everything to be easy."

They had reached the northern side of the terrace. No groups of people had collected here, perhaps because no tables of food and drink had been set up at this end of the terrace. Teressa was silent as she stared at the forested land beyond the city, then turned to face him.

"There's something out there, Captain." She looked north again and pointed across the forest to the far plain. "I am now convinced of it. There is something out there that didn't reveal itself during the first years of our presence here, except in the nightmares of many people. I had such dreams myself as a child, and so did my parents and some of the people they knew, and then the dreaming stopped." She spoke so calmly that he could almost believe that she was not truly afraid. "But it's getting worse now."

"Exactly what do you mean?" Kirk asked. "Are you talking about a disease of some kind, perhaps an indigenous virus or native bacterium?"

"No, nothing like that. We had such problems in the beginning, and we still have to be very careful with any unfamiliar plant and animal life, although we've catalogued almost all of the species on this continent. Merope Four has its share of plants that are poisonous and reptiles and insects that are potentially deadly to humans, but this isn't anything like that."

She paused. "You have our report on the settlement that disappeared."

Kirk nodded. "My science officer has been studying your audio and visual records, but he says we'll have to go to the site ourselves to learn anything about possible causes."

She looked up at him, searching his face. "I thought that this was just an isolated incident. I was thinking of asking for your help, but I was hoping that we'd find some obvious explanation by now, or that you might, and that would be the end of it. Now—"

Teressa sighed. "Before that settlement disappeared," she continued, "people there were having dreams—the same dream. Several people in Shaku and New Ibadan were also dreaming the same nightmare. Then the settlement was engulfed, and the dreams stopped. Now people are having the same dreams again, both in this city and in Shaku."

"And what about your other towns and villages?" Kirk asked.

"A member of the Bakundi town council contacted me this morning, about children sleeping badly there and reporting bad dreams to their parents. This councilman said he'd been having such dreams, too. Bakundi is only three hundred kilometers to our south, on the other side of the Temba River. I don't know about any other communities yet, and frankly I'm wary of asking. I don't want to alarm people unnecessarily, but the fears of many people are increasing, especially in Shaku. Captain—"

She fell silent for several moments, and Kirk knew that she was anxious to be precise in what she was about to say. He glanced around and saw that no one was standing near them. "Go on," he murmured.

"Captain Kirk, I suspect that we may be dealing with . . . with a kind of life-form."

"What evidence do you have for your suspicions?" he asked.

"The nightmares. They match—the people who have these dreams have the same dream, over and over. Dawn

Voth did some discreet investigation yesterday, and she reports that people all over New Ibadan are dreaming identical dreams. As an old saying goes, people do not dream in unison."

"No, under normal circumstances, they don't," Kirk said. "What do they . . . what do you dream?"

"Of being engulfed, taken over, put into a state of personal forgetfulness. It's like a creeping kind of amnesia. You feel as though you may lose yourself entirely before you wake up. I have to struggle to wake up, work at getting out of my dream. Others report the same sensation. It's like a sea that keeps washing into my mind when I sleep, threatening to drown all the little places where I am aware of myself, until only a silence is left, and an acceptance of something else that will no longer be me."

Kirk looked into her hazel eyes and saw a mixture of sober judgment and fear.

"I fear now," she continued, "that there may be no solution to this problem, and if that's the case, we may be at an end here. I did not want to say that to you except privately. We've accepted the people from the *Hawking* as colonists, but please keep in mind that we may not be able to do much for ourselves or for anyone else if this becomes a serious problem. I need your help, but now I'm not sure what you can do for us. It may be that you'll have to contact Starfleet and ask for the rapid evacuation and relocation of all our people." A sigh escaped her. "This is the only world I know. It would pain me so to have to leave it."

"I appreciate your frankness, First Citizen," Kirk said,

"and don't jump to any conclusions about what might happen."

"I'll try not to."

"I am going to send some of my personnel to the location of the settlement that disappeared, as Mr. Spock recommended. We'll see what they can find out."

Her lips formed a smile, but a strange, haunted look had come into her lovely face, as if the unknown was again pushing into her, and he wondered if she had possessed this beauty before the intrusion

Chapter Eight

"REALLY, TERESSA," Trent said, "you might have told me before."

"I am telling you now," Teressa replied. She had gone to her aide's quarters after the reception was over and the new colonists had gone off to their new homes with their Meropean host families. Trent had left the reception early. She had seen him strolling around the plaza, arm in arm with Lieutenant Uhura, before the young woman had left him there to return to the party on the terrace. Trent had glared angrily after Uhura when she was walking away; Teressa wondered why, but would not ask. She had already guessed that her aide had known Uhura back on Earth, and perhaps their past relationship had been more than a simple friendship.

"You needn't have prevailed upon Captain Kirk for any assistance," Trent said.

"He offered to help us. He wants to help."

"Making him aware of our problem would have been quite enough. I don't see how he and his personnel can help us with this . . . mystery."

"Maybe they can't," Teressa replied, "but we might as well make use of them and their resources while they're here."

"Starfleet," Trent said disdainfully. His cat Banta, an indigenous creature with thick black and white fur, and slightly larger than one of Earth's domestic cats, glared up at Teressa with fierce green eyes that looked as angry as Trent's brown ones. "Starfleet's too far away to know our particular circumstances and be able to decide what's right for us to do. There's no point in dragging them into this until you're certain you need their help."

"Captain Kirk is willing to help us and has resources we lack, along with officers and a crew with training we don't have. It would be foolish not to take advantage of that. I don't know what you've got against Starfleet, Trent."

He did not respond right away. "You are the First Citizen," he said at last. "You must do what you think is best."

"Yes, I must," she said more gently, "and I'll need your advice and support, too."

"You have that, Teressa. You always will. Just don't put too much faith in Starfleet. They can also make mistakes."

Spock had beamed down with Lieutenant Sulu and Dr. McCoy to the site of the destroyed settlement. As soon as the world around Spock was steady, he noted where the town had been.

The site was all dry mud flats now. The fissures had closed. There was no sign of human habitation left. He lifted his eyes to the distant hills bordering the plain. The slopes were covered with the dark green of trees that resembled pines, along with yellow and blue swatches of wildflowers. The desolation of the flat and barren site contrasted markedly with the profusion of life on the land around it.

"Damn," McCoy muttered under his breath. Spock knew what the medical officer was thinking; against all reason, Dr. McCoy had undoubtedly hoped to find survivors.

Behind them, in the east, the sun was rising, casting a soft pinkish light over the ground. Spock led the way forward across the site, checking his tricorder readings. Sulu walked at his left, McCoy at his right; both men seemed uneasy. He continued his scan until they came to the edge that divided the dry mud flats from the grassy meadow that surrounded them.

No natural event, Spock thought, was likely to have produced such a sharply defined border between the dry ground of the destroyed settlement and the green surrounding land. The corrosive effects on the surface seemed quite evident. The human constructions that had been here were manifest only from the residue of destruction by acids. The sticky brownish lumps and patches on the ground, according to his readings, indicated that the dwellings in the settlement had been made of wood. There was no evidence of human bodies at all, so they had to have been buried very deeply.

Spock paused to examine more of his tricorder readings. "There seem to have been electrical effects of an unknown origin," he said. "Curious."

"They're gone," McCoy said. "How they went won't help us now. One hundred and seven people are just gone."

"Calm yourself, Doctor," Spock said. "What we learn here may prevent it from happening again."

"I'll contact the captain and give him a report," Sulu said as he took out his communicator and flipped it open. "Sulu to *Enterprise*. Come in, *Enterprise*."

"Kirk here," the captain's voice replied. "What have you got?"

"Not much, sir," Sulu said. "There's nothing left here except mud flats. The only evidence that there was a settlement here at all is a residue indicating that wooden structures once stood on this site."

As Spock listened to Sulu give his report on what they had observed, he began to feel unsettled, almost as if something was probing at his mind. He glanced at McCoy. The physician also seemed disturbed by something more than his usually commendable concern for human welfare.

"Dr. McCoy," Spock said, "is something bothering you?"

McCoy quickly shook his head. "Not at all," he answered, but the way he had responded indicated that he was more troubled than he wanted to admit.

"Then I must tell you," Spock said, "that I feel extremely uneasy at the moment, almost as if some invisible life-form or being is present and attempting to provoke fear." He was silent for a moment, and now it seemed as though the presence was attempting to unravel some of his thoughts. "No, that is not quite accurate. It is more a sensation of something trying to pull at various strands of knowledge and memory inside me."

McCoy's eyes widened. "That's it—that's exactly the way I feel, like something's trying to steal my thoughts." The doctor looked both relieved and apprehensive. "You feel it, too?"

"Yes, Dr. McCoy."

Sulu turned toward them. "Then that makes three of us," the lieutenant muttered. "Right now, I'm—I don't know quite how to phrase it. I'm trying to hang on to parts of myself."

Spock flipped open his communicator. "Captain," he said, "Spock here. There is now some evidence that we may be dealing with an unseen alien life-form, something that may be intelligent, and that might have deliberately destroyed this Meropean community. I sense a strange presence clearly, and so do Dr. McCoy and Lieutenant Sulu."

"Jim," McCoy added, "I think—"

Spock suddenly felt a trembling under his feet. A quake, he thought, and then saw a crack open in the ground a hundred meters in front of him. Just as he registered that fact, the crack was racing east toward him. Before it reached him, he jumped to his left, then saw McCoy leap after him.

"Good Lord!" McCoy gasped. Spock looked around

and noticed that Sulu was trapped on the other side of a chasm now too wide to leap across. The crack was still running east; it ran on for another one hundred meters and then stopped.

"What now?" Sulu shouted from the other side of the opening.

Spock approached the fissure and looked down, taking new readings with his tricorder. Deep inside the crack, a green mass was forming. Fascinating, he thought as he watched a green grass-like mass rise out of the crevasse and creep toward his feet. He stepped back and the mass rose higher.

He retreated from the burgeoning mossy substance, with McCoy at his side. It was growing fast; the green wall was already taller than a man. Sulu was no longer visible on the other side.

"Mr. Sulu!" Spock called out, and then the mass began to slide toward him.

"Jim!" McCoy said into his communicator as he and Spock retreated. "Beam us out of here right now! And get Sulu—he's about a hundred meters away from us."

As Spock awaited rescue, he and the doctor continued to retreat from the green wall, which was now some seven meters high and seemed to be all of an endless piece rising from the crack. More fissures formed in the ground; Spock leaped over a crack as it ran past him.

"This wall," McCoy was saying, "this mass . . . it's what destroyed the town."

"I am well aware of that, Doctor," Spock said, peering at his tricorder.

* * *

"It's a living thing, Jim," McCoy's voice said from the comm. "It's coming right at us."

On the bridge, Kirk leaned forward at his station. "Beam them up, Scotty," he ordered.

"Aye," the chief engineer replied. "Just give me a moment to lock on."

"A living thing," McCoy's voice continued, "and possibly intelligent, according to Spock," and then Kirk heard the sound of a man gasping for breath.

"Bones," Kirk said, "are you all right?"

"Yes, Jim, but we've got to move even faster now. We're running, more cracks are forming, and it's still—"

"Captain, we've got them!" Scotty called out from the transporter room.

"What about Sulu?" Kirk asked.

"We have him, too, looking only slightly the worse for wear."

Kirk let out a sigh of relief. "Send them all up to the bridge."

"Aye, Captain, they're on their way."

As Kirk waited at his command station, he realized that the situation was about to get much more complicated than he had expected. Only a few days ago, he had been planning to get Leander Cortés and his shipmates settled on Merope IV and then go on to his next mission—spacedock for the *Enterprise* and an extended leave on Earth for his crew. Even Teresa Aliss's talk of synchronous dreaming and the mysterious menace that had swallowed a whole town had not unduly alarmed him; he had been hoping that a thorough tricorder scan of the doomed settlement's site and a fresh look at the problem might reveal a quick solution.

But that hope was quickly fading. The *Enterprise* was going to be here longer than he had planned.

The sun was well above the horizon by the time Teressa left her quarters to go down to her office. Trent was waiting for her, and he had brought his cat with him. The animal was crouched at his feet, her head resting on her front paws.

"You got up much later than usual," Trent said.

"I know." Teressa went to her desk and sat down. "It's that dream again—it was much worse last night. I couldn't get out of it, I couldn't wake up, and when I finally did, I was frightened."

"I dreamed it, too," Trent said. "I woke up when it was still dark, I was afraid to go back to sleep. I could hear Nguyen's baby crying next door, he was shrieking for at least an hour, he wouldn't stop. Then Banta started howling—screeching. She's never done that before."

Teressa regarded the cat. Normally she would get a cold green-eyed stare in return. This time, Banta squinted at her and let out a piteous mewing sound. "Is that why you brought her here?" she asked.

"Banta wouldn't let me leave my quarters without her. She grabbed on to my trouser leg with her claws and wouldn't let go. I finally freed myself and brought her down to the courtyard, but she refuses to go outside."

Teressa thumbed her screen. Four messages were waiting for her. She leaned toward the screen and listened to them quickly. Messanga Watson had several reports from residents of Shaku, about nightmares and about disturbances among their domestic animals. A member of the Gombé town council reported that large flocks of waterfowl had been seen flying toward the Kainji Mountains, in defiance of their usual migratory patterns at this time of year. Dawn Voth had sent a message saying that households all over New Ibadan were complaining about children terrified by bad dreams, adults who had awakened with temporary losses of memory, and pets that had howled throughout the night. The last message was from Captain James T. Kirk, informing her that Commander Spock, Dr. Leonard McCoy, and Lieutenant Hikaru Sulu had beamed down to the site of the settlement that had disappeared, and that he would report any findings to her later.

"Teressa," Trent said, "I—"

Banta suddenly stood up on her four legs, arched her back, and meowed. Teressa could hear another sound outside, a sound like that of many distant voices. She got up and went to the window and glass doors that faced the Yakuru Plaza.

Hundreds of people had gathered at the western end of the plaza. Across the way, outside the Alim al-Reyhan Primary School, men and women were holding small children in their arms or trying to calm others who were clearly frightened. As Teressa watched, more people flooded into the square.

"What's going on?" she whispered.

A chime sounded from behind her. She hurried back to her desk and thumbed her screen.

The image of Dawn Voth appeared. "Teressa," the councilwoman said, "we've got trouble—big trouble."

Spock left the lift and came onto the bridge, followed by McCoy and Sulu. Kirk motioned to them from his station. "Spock," he called out, "what did you mean before when you mentioned an intelligent life-form?"

Spock seemed about to reply when Uhura turned toward Kirk from her station. "Captain," she said abruptly, "an emergency call is coming in from First Citizen Teressa Aliss."

Kirk leaned forward. "Put her on the screen, Lieutenant."

Teressa Aliss's worried face appeared. Behind her, he glimpsed Trent Ojuremi and Dawn Voth. "Captain Kirk," the First Citizen said, "we have an emergency on our hands. We need help. Fissures started opening up around New Ibadan early this morning. Now large grassy mats and waves of green moss are coming up from the ground and beginning to move toward the city."

"How far away?" Kirk asked.

"According to reports, approximately twenty kilometers, but the matted material seems to be moving at about five kilometers an hour. It's already clearly visible on the other side of the Temba River, and fingers of grass are slipping into the river, as if trying to form a bridge from the southern bank over to New Ibadan itself."

Kirk glanced at Spock and saw that his first officer had something to tell him, but was holding back.

"We have some of our civic patrols out now," the First Citizen continued, "trying to calm people, but we almost had a riot on our hands here, in the plaza. We're trying to get people to return to their homes for the moment, and wait, but—" She shook her head. "What are we going to do?"

"Spock," Kirk said, "whatever you have to tell me, say it now. Ms. Aliss should hear it, too."

"Captain," the Vulcan said, "I believe we are dealing with what I can only describe as a kind of neural net—a creature that is all nervous system and may even be as large as the surface land area of Merope Four, perhaps even larger than that. My supposition is that it seems to have existed inside the planetary crust, but is now coming out."

"But why would it come out?" Kirk asked.

Spock lifted an eyebrow and shrugged. "Perhaps up until now, there were not enough alien nervous systems present to disturb the net. But the steadily increasing population may have created a disturbance, while our arrival may have made intruders evident to this organism."

"In effect," McCoy said, "we're only just now showing up on its radar."

Spock nodded. "That is both picturesque and accurate, Doctor."

"But is it intelligent?" Teressa Aliss asked. She did not wait for a reply. "Dreams—many of us here were dreaming again, Captain, troubled by the same dreams I mentioned to you at the reception. The dreams—maybe that was this neural net trying to warn us, or trying to frighten us away. But we didn't leave, and now—can it be intelligent? Is it possible that—" Her voice trailed off.

"It is difficult to say, First Citizen," Spock replied. "It

is possible that such a net might simply be responding with what could be a kind of reflex action, with no conscious thought. But it is difficult for me to imagine that such a large net would not have its own kind of intelligence. The size of its system alone suggests a richness—"

"Mr. Spock," Teressa Aliss interrupted, "whatever it is, it will engulf our city from all sides in some twenty-four hours at its present rate. We are surrounded."

Chapter Nine

DMITRI GLAKOV had followed him to the plaza, trailed by Emo Tannan and Rachel Zlatopolsky. By the time Leander Cortés was climbing the steps to the terrace, others from the *Hawking* had come to join him.

Five young men and women, wearing what Cortés recognized as the light blue shirts of the New Ibadan civic patrol, stood at the top of the steps. "Go back to your homes," one of the young men said. "We're asking people to go back to their homes or workplaces and to wait there."

"We'll head back," Cortés said. "We just want to take a look at what's going on from the terrace."

The young man's eyes shifted slightly. "You're some of the new arrivals, aren't you? The people from the old spaceship."

Cortés nodded. "Yes. Your people took us in. Now maybe we can return the favor by helping you out somehow."

The man glanced at his companions, then stepped aside. "All right, old-timer, but don't stay up here too long. We don't want people trying to get from the outer parts of the city into the central areas, and they may try to if they get frightened enough. They'd come flooding back into the plaza then, and up to the terrace, thinking they might be safer here."

"We'll just take a quick look," Cortés said.

Two days, he thought to himself as he strode toward the southern end of the terrace, one day for the reception and party and another day to get acquainted with their hosts, and now they were facing a crisis he did not understand on an alien world he did not know.

He came to the edge of the terrace and saw that at least fifty of his shipmates had followed him here. Perhaps some had guessed that he might come here, where the Meropean leader had welcomed them, while others might simply have decided to head toward the center of the city, but seeing them all there reassured him. They were his comrades; he had seen them at their best and at their worst and he knew that he could rely on them now. Hope had flowered in them once more after they had left their ship, and he was not about to let it die again.

Cortés looked south. On the other side of the river, he saw an unbroken horizon of mossy green. The house where he was staying, owned by a man named Kembo Turner, was in the northern section of New Ibadan, near the top of one of the city's gentle hills. He and Kembo had been able to see a green, grassy wall in the distance. It looked like it was slowly growing—or flowing—toward the city. The green wall across the river was closer, and green tendrils were already growing across the water.

Emo Tannan came to his side. "We're surrounded," Emo murmured. "This city's surrounded on all sides by that—that stuff."

Cortés nodded, then turned toward the group. "Yesterday," he said, "my host Kembo Turner took me on a short tour near the city's outskirts. He showed me some of the land vehicles and some of the equipment the farmers here use for clearing new fields. I thought their machinery would be a lot more advanced than it is, but then this is a colony world that still lacks many of the more advanced tools of their Federation. Kembo taught me how to drive and handle one of the vehicles in less than half an hour."

"Leander, exactly what are you trying to say?" Rachel asked.

"I'm saying that if we can get ourselves equipped with some vehicles and heavy-duty phasers—that's what the Meropeans use to clear overgrown land—we might be able to help turn back the green tide."

"*We* might be able to?" Nasser al-Aswari said.

"Yes." Cortés glanced from one face to another. "These people could use some help. We've all stared into the abyss when we were aboard the *Hawking,* knowing that we were on a dead ship—facing this is nothing compared to that. I think we should go to First Citizen Aliss and offer her our services."

For a moment, as they all stared at him in silence, he thought they might protest. They had just arrived here; this was not their world; the people here were still strangers. They had been promised a new start, not a new battle to wage. A civilization that could command the kind of power and technology they had seen aboard the *Enterprise* could easily transport them to another planet. They had been through enough, and owed the people of Merope IV nothing.

"I'll volunteer," Emo Tannan said.

Rachel Zlatopolsky stepped forward. "So will I," she said.

"Count me in, too," Laure Vidor cried out. "I've also learned how to drive one of those vehicles."

"And I'm willing to come along," Dmitri Glakov said, and then others were calling out to him, and Cortés knew that they were all in agreement with him. They were ready to fight at his side.

As he gazed at Teressa Aliss's grim expression on the viewscreen, Kirk saw the determination that had made her the leader among her people. Yet there was also something else in her face, a prescient uneasiness that almost seemed to have expected and anticipated the onset of a planetary problem for her colony.

He reminded himself that living with the biology of an alien world, however Earthlike, always posed dangers to the biology of invaders. The evolutionary match was impossible, however parallel, and precautions had to be taken, adjustments had to be made.

Something on Merope IV, something natural to that world, was now making its own adjustments.

"We're scanning the area around New Ibadan," Kirk said, then turned aft toward Spock. "What does the scan show?"

"A moment, Captain," Spock said.

Kirk turned forward again to face Teressa Aliss's eyes. She gazed back at him without blinking, and then he heard the sound of someone else calling out to her. She rose quickly, leaning against her desk as she looked to her left at something offscreen.

"What's going on?" Kirk asked.

Aliss lifted a hand. "I'll be right with you, Captain." Kirk saw Trent Ojuremi cross the room behind her. "Captain Cortés is here," the First Citizen continued, "and he says he has something very important to ask me. I'll see what he wants and get back to you."

Kirk nodded. "Lieutenant Uhura," he said, "keep this channel open." Aliss had left her desk; he recognized the voice of Leander Cortés in the background, but could not make out what the Earthman was saying.

"Maintaining contact, sir," Uhura said.

The First Citizen reappeared on the screen. "Captain Kirk," she said, "I have just received a rather remarkable proposal from Captain Cortés, namely that we arm about a dozen of his people with phasers and send them out in a few of our land vehicles . . . to mow the lawn, as he puts it. He says that he already knows how to drive a land vehicle himself—someone in his host family showed him how—and he's convinced that his comrades who haven't driven them yet can learn just as quickly."

The image of Cortés appeared next to her. "It's true," the captain of the *Hawking* added. "Much easier than driving a tank, or a truck, and the phasers seem simple enough to handle."

Kirk felt a surge of admiration for the man. "Are you sure you want to do this?"

"Captain Kirk, when you found us, you brought dead men and women back to life. We have been living on borrowed time ever since. Rather than hoarding that time, we should spend it helping these people who welcomed us to their world." Cortés's lips formed a half-smile. "In any event, none of us will have a home here if we don't stop this growth somehow. I insist—maybe this is all it will take to stop it."

"Captain Kirk," Aliss asked, "what are your thoughts? Is this worth trying?"

"I think it is. I commend Captain Cortés and his people for their offer." Kirk looked aft. "Your opinion, Mr. Spock."

"It is possible," the Vulcan said from his station, "that a thinning may cause the front to pause, and perhaps even to retreat. I do not recommend using an overwhelming force at first, until we determine if lesser force is enough to retard the advance of this green growth, or even to stop it."

"Isn't there anything you and your ship can do to help?" the First Citizen asked.

"I'm going to send a couple of my officers down there," Kirk replied, "to aid Cortés's operation and gather whatever data they can. We'll also continue our sensor scan and keep watch from up here. If Cortés and his comrades are endangered, we'll beam them up to safety immediately." He would not let them go out to fight without doing everything possible to protect them. "And then we'll use more force against this threat if we have to."

114

Teressa Aliss glanced to her left. "Trent," she said, "requisition seven vehicles and give Captain Cortés and his people some very fast training. See that the vehicles are equipped with tripod-mounted industrial or agricultural phasers and that each person going out is given a hand-held phaser and shown how to use it."

"Done," Trent Ojuremi's voice replied. "Captain Cortés, come with me."

"Ms. Aliss," Spock said, "I would advise the use of phasers set for heavy stun, to see whether the matted growth pauses or retreats. Disruption mode should be used only as a last resort."

"But why?" Aliss asked. "What kind of counsel is that? This entire city is threatened!"

"That's true," Kirk said, "but we may be dealing with a planetary intelligence. If we can find a way to stop it, there may also be ways to get it to leave you alone in the future. But if it feels its existence threatened, it may become even more destructive in self-defense."

Teressa Aliss's hazel eyes narrowed with anger and disdain. Kirk realized that she was considering only the survival of New Ibadan. Whether or not the aggressor was intelligent or simply part of a mindless ecological response to alien human life would make no difference if destruction became necessary.

"Very well," she said. "We'll do it your way, for now."

Chekov turned toward Kirk. "Captain," the Russian said, "I will volunteer to beam down to the surface."

"I'd like to go, too," Uhura said.

"Captain . . ." Sulu began.

Kirk stood up. "Yes, I know. All of you would—I know

that." He turned aft. "Chekov and Longstreet—I'm sending both of you down to the surface. Your orders are to stay with Cortés and do whatever you can to assist him." He longed to beam down there himself to lead the fight, but his place was on the bridge until he learned more about this menace, and how it might be stopped.

Chekov stood near Trent Ojuremi as the Meropean instructed several of Captain Cortés's companions on driving the land vehicles, which resembled small tanks enclosed in transparent carapaces. Another man, a city councilman named Muhammad Alagbe, handed out hand phasers to each of the volunteers who would be stationed along the riverbank, with members of the New Ibadan civic patrol, to fire at any mats of growth on the opposite bank in order to prevent the greenery from spreading across the water.

That job, Chekov thought, was probably the easier one. He and Farley Longstreet, on the other hand, would be following Cortés in one of the vehicles. Cortés would lead the vehicular charge, and had selected those who would come with him by the time Alagbe had finished instructing everyone in the operation of the heavy mounted phasers. Chekov and Longstreet, following Captain Kirk's orders, would allow the *Hawking*'s captain the dignity of commanding his own people, but they would be ready to take over should that prove necessary.

There would be two people in each vehicle, one to drive and one to fire the weapon; Longstreet would man the phaser in Chekov's vehicle. Emo Tannan was going with Cortés; Rachel Zlatopolsky and Dmitri Glakov would take a second vehicle. Laure Vidor would take the third, with Nasser al-Aswari to man the mounted phaser in that vehicle; Xavier Rodriguez and Anthony Tikriti would be in a fourth. Several Meropeans had wanted to join the group, but Cortés had refused their offer.

"Let us be your front line," the captain of the *Hawking* had told them. "If we fail, you will have to carry on the fight—but perhaps we will not fail."

Seven vehicles in all, and fourteen people in them—Chekov fervently hoped that would be enough to keep the city from being overwhelmed. If they fell, other volunteers, Meropeans and others from the *Hawking,* would have to follow them, with more officers from the *Enterprise* to watch out for them—but he would not think of that now.

"Any questions?" Muhammad Alagbe asked after he had finished giving his quick course of instruction in phaser use.

"Better ask them now," Trent Ojuremi added.

Everyone was silent. "No," Cortés said at last.

"Then it is time to mow the lawn!" Glakov shouted. Chekov lifted his arm and saluted his kinsman.

The land vehicles moved out of the western end of the city. Through the clear protective covering of his vehicle, and on the small viewscreen next to his controls, Cortés saw an advancing green wall of mossy growth on the horizon in all directions. The matted wall surrounded the city, and it was now less than twelve kilometers away.

Emo sat in the rear compartment, at the controls of the large phaser that had been mounted on a tripod attached to the carapace. Aiming and firing the weapon was a simple matter; the automatic controls took care of just about everything. Alagbe had told them that both the hand-held phasers and the large mounted ones were simple enough for small children to handle—not that anyone on Merope IV would ever have allowed small children near them.

But there was a difference between using the phasers to clear land and aiming them at an enemy alien, a *thing* that might swallow you. Cortés thought of the bacteria and mildew that had begun to spread through the *Hawking* before they had found a way to rid themselves of the growth. To this alien Meropean life, perhaps human beings were little more than a kind of infestation, something to be scoured and scrubbed away.

The plan was to circle the city, moving north and then east, while firing at the leading edge of the incoming green mass—first on stun, and then on disrupt if necessary. Teressa Aliss had been very clear about her order, repeating it over the comm just before the vehicles rolled out of New Ibadan, and both of the young officers from the *Enterprise* had concurred with her. The order struck Cortés as too cautious, but he was determined to carry it out to the letter. He and his people would prove their commitment to their future place in this colony by defending it.

Cortés's vehicle moved forward, leading the other six. When they were a thousand meters away from the growth, he leaned toward the panel in front of him, made sure that the comm was still open, and said, "Commence firing."

The heavy phasers fired, sending stun bolts into the tall

mats. Even inside the closed cab of his vehicle, and through the earphones of his headset, the sound assaulted his ears; it was a whooping cry that snapped like a whip as the bolts found their mark. He marveled at the energies contained in the small power packs, and in the even smaller hand-held phasers he and his people now wore on their belts.

They kept moving, continuing to fire at the green wall on their left as they went north and then east. Cortés could not see if the phaser fire had halted the growth. He and his people rolled on until they reached the eastern side of the city, and then drove south, toward the river. By the time he glimpsed the river through the trees, he was certain that they had failed in their assault on the green wall.

"Slow down, comrades," he ordered through his comm link. "The river's up ahead." Through the trees, he saw a green wall on the opposite bank, and what looked like small islands of moss floating on the water.

"We do not seem to be making any progress," Ensign Chekov's voice said from his headset.

"How are we doing, Ms. Aliss?" Cortés asked.

"I'm afraid you'll have to try again, Captain Cortés," the First Citizen's voice replied. "Head back the way you came, and keep firing."

"Order acknowledged," Cortés muttered. "Everyone, we're going to retrace our route once more. I'm turning around now—follow me, and continue to fire on stun!"

His vehicle picked up speed. A display panel on the controls told him that they were maintaining a distance of a thousand meters between vehicles. The bolts shot into the green wall again, but he could not tell if the phaser fire was having any results.

"What's the word, First Citizen?" he asked as he turned west. "Are we accomplishing anything at all?"

"We should know in a few moments," Aliss replied. "The *Enterprise* is scanning now."

As he and the others went on firing, Cortés looked out at the great grassy twisting mass to his right. It sat on the land, a green wall that had come out of the ground, weeds consuming this world, worse than any nightmare he had dreamed in his three decades aboard the *Hawking*. Maybe he was still asleep there, dreaming this horror.

No, he told himself, there was one difference. In his shipboard dreams, he had been given no weapons with which to defend himself. Here, he was armed, and possibly doing some good—both for his comrades and for others.

Uhura sat at her station, keeping the channels between the *Enterprise* and the city of New Ibadan open and on standby. Trent, she knew, had gone back to the city council offices to wait with Teressa Aliss.

At her left, Commander Spock was studying the display of the latest scans. The Vulcan looked up and then turned toward the captain's command station. "Captain," he said, "the attack carried out twice now by Captain Cortés and his volunteers has had no effect."

Captain Kirk stood up and came aft to Spock's station.

"You can see there," Spock continued, pointing to the display, "that there has been no sign that the green biomass has retreated, or even come to a temporary halt. It is still moving toward the outskirts of the city."

Captain Kirk sighed. "Uhura, get me Teressa Aliss."

"The channel's still open, sir." Uhura pressed a button on her console. "I'm hailing her now."

What would happen to the people in the city? she thought. Even if the crew of the *Enterprise* tried to beam them to safer places away from New Ibadan, there would not be enough time to rescue them all. There were also not enough shuttlecraft to ferry them all away from Merope IV. Even if rescue and relocation in other regions of the planet were possible, Uhura wondered if that would do any good. The hungry wall of weeds might only rise up from the ground to attack elsewhere.

The captain went back to his station as the forward viewscreen lit up, revealing the image of Teressa Aliss.

"I've got bad news," Kirk said.

Her mouth twisted. "Your face has already delivered that news, Captain Kirk," the First Citizen said in a hoarse and weary voice. "You are going to tell me that Captain Cortés's operation has had no effect."

"Yes," he said. "Time to tell Cortés to go to disruption. Tell him and his people to set their phasers to the maximum setting."

"I'll give the order," she said.

Uhura could see Trent's shadowy form behind Aliss's. "Teressa," he said, "mats of green stuff are drifting across the river toward the riverfront." Uhura heard his words very clearly. "We'd better withdraw the patrol groups there before it reaches them."

The viewscreen winked out. Kirk turned toward Uhura. "Lieutenant Uhura," he said, "I need an officer with Ms. Aliss now, someone to keep our communications open to her and to advise her if she needs advice. I'm not sure how much we can rely on her aide under the circumstances, and since you know him, you might be able to— keep things there under control."

Uhura stood up. "I'm sending you down to New Ibadan," the captain went on, "and your orders are to stay with the First Citizen."

"Yes, sir." She hurried toward the turbolift.

They were back where they had started, outside the west end of the city. Through his headset, Chekov heard Cortés order his people to set their mounted phasers to disruption. That had to mean that Captain Kirk had already informed the First Citizen that their attacks had failed.

Cortés's vehicle led the way north again; Chekov followed, keeping the captain's vehicle in sight. As the vehicles accelerated, it looked to him as though the wall had moved closer. He peered at the control display; his heart sank as it confirmed his observation.

"It's a lot closer, isn't it, friends?" Emo Tannan's voice said inside Chekov's headset. "That's what you're all thinking, isn't it?"

"Damn right it is," Cortés's voice replied. "You're a mind reader, Emo."

"And I've got eyes. That green stuff's still out of control—I can see it. Phaser set to disruption."

"Everyone," Cortés said, "also set your hand phaser settings to disruption."

Someone chuckled. "Hell, Leander," Rachel Zlatopolsky's voice said, "if we need to use our hand phasers, we'd have to get out of these bubbletop trucks to fire them. How do we manage that without getting that green stuff all over us in the meantime?"

"You're an engineer, Rachel," the voice of another woman said. "Figure something out."

"I'm an engineer, not a gardener, and this stuff could use a mighty powerful weedkiller."

The phasers opened up, and now Chekov saw a different effect. A strange blue light blazed at his left, and he knew that vast sections of the mat were simply disappearing into thin air as the attack group trimmed the perimeter.

"Well, what do you know," Farley Longstreet said over Chekov's headset from his place in the back of their vehicle. "I think we're finally getting rid of some weeds."

The phasers were doing their job, Cortés thought; the attack was at last having some results.

"Captain Cortés," a voice said in his ear, "this is Commander Spock. The mat seems to have launched a wave of organic material in the direction of your vehicles. If you can decrease your speed immediately by ten kilometers an hour, the wave will strike ground ahead of you."

"Thanks, Commander," Cortés said. "All vehicles, slow your speed by ten klicks per hour, now!"

As he peered to his left across the plain that separated the vehicles from the green wall, Cortés saw a great cloud sweeping toward him in an arc. As it came closer, he saw that it was composed of conelike units, and was reminded of the pine trees of his Canadian childhood, and how they would cover the grass with their cones. As the alien cones struck the ground, a sickly blue mist rose from them.

Acid, he thought as the sterile, cleared land under the cones turned yellow and then black under the thick blue mist. He slowed his vehicle to a stop and waited, watching as the mist thickened and burned the land. The planet was striking back, he realized. It was taking back the terrain around the alien city.

The ground trembled under his vehicle. "Quake!" Emo said from behind him. He peered out and saw nothing, and then the ground shook again.

"Leander!" That was Rachel. "The ground is opening!"

Cortés looked out once more and saw cracks in the ground running toward his vehicle. In another moment, he felt the planet yawn below him.

His vehicle plunged downward, scraping against the sides of a crevasse, then stopped suddenly with a jolt that nearly cracked his head against the carapace, and he knew that he was lodged in the narrows of the opening.

Ahead of him, he saw nothing but rock and dirt. He looked to his right and saw a long narrow canyon. Dusty daylight came in from above, and all was still. Then he realized that Emo was awfully quiet.

"Emo," he called out. "Emo!"

When there was no answer, he hoisted himself from his seat and peered down into the rear compartment. Emo was slumped forward over his phaser control panel, his head twisted to one side. Cortés feared that the other man's neck had been broken during the fall.

"Emo!" he shouted. "Move a hand, a finger, something."

Still there was no answer or movement. Cortés suspected that his vehicle was not going to move again. He looked down the canyon again, and this time saw a dark green mass moving toward him. It came on rapidly as he watched, and in a moment the clear carapace protecting him was being covered. A strange hiss sounded from outside, and he realized that the mass was beginning to use its acids to eat through the vehicle.

He pressed his hand against his control panel. *"Enterprise,"* he said as calmly as he could, "this is Cortés. I'm trapped in a crevasse, and I think Emo Tannan, my gunner, is seriously injured." He refused to believe his friend was dead, not yet. "Our vehicle is stuck in this crevasse, and a green mass is flowing around us trying to swallow us."

"Kirk here," the starship captain's voice said in his ear. "Mr. Spock tells me that the acids secreted by the mass are eating through your vehicle. How is your life support?"

"I'm breathing," Cortés replied, "but it does feel colder in here." He thought of his companions. "Comrades," he went on, "if you can hear me now, respond." There was no answer. "Respond!"

He waited, then let out his breath. "No answer, Captain Kirk. My comrades aren't responding—neither are your officers. I suspect that their vehicles may also be trapped in the running cracks, and that they're either dead or unable to answer."

"We'll get you out of there. Is there any way you can climb out of your vehicle and get to the surface?"

"No, I can't! Damn it, Kirk, this stuff is all around me and eating through! There's no way out!"

As he spoke, his interior lights went out, leaving him in total darkness.

"My lights are out now," he said. "Can't even see my hand. Are you still there?"

"Still with you," Kirk said more faintly, "we're scanning now, we'll get . . ." and then his voice broke up and Cortés was left in a silent gloom. He sat very still and listened, knowing that this would be his end. He had come decades and light years from Earth, only to be eaten alive by a bunch of moss.

He laughed in the darkness, just to hear his own voice in the awful silence, but the laughter was even worse than the quiet. He fell silent again, listening to the soft whisper of the green mass, as it ate its way toward him through a shell that centuries of technical progress had not made immune to the adaptive acids of the alien life-form.

He would not see the end. He would hear the mass come through the carapace, and he would feel it engulf his body. Would he die instantly, or would he be embedded in the mass for some time, being digested, perhaps probed?

Cortés was suddenly startled to hear his own involuntary screaming. It started and rose to a high pitch and went on in the darkness. He found himself listening to it as if it were someone else—a fellow human being who had cracked, had become more than one integral personality. His other self was revolting against the iron discipline of the one who had commanded and guided a starship across the dark and not flinched. Well, that other Leander can be as stoic as he wishes, the screamer said, but I am not going down quietly. . . .

But after a few moments, the screamer shut down, and Cortés had the feeling that a part of him had died. He did not feel that it was a mercy.

He closed his eyes in the darkness and almost laughed at the absurdity of doing so; and for a moment it seemed to him that he was back aboard the *Hawking,* in his sleep cubicle, wrestling with the intractability of light-years that could not be overcome, thinking of the green mold that was growing again in parts of the air system, and how to clean it out before it became a dangerous disease of some kind. . . .

But the air ducts had been cleaned out, he recalled, opening his eyes wide in the darkness, as if somehow he might pick up something and light the back of his brain. Emo had crawled through the ducts, scouring with disinfectant, wiping at the stuff with rags, coughing and grunting, until the job was done.

Emo.

Cortés reached for his hand phaser, pressed it to his heart, and waited.

Chapter Ten

MONTGOMERY SCOTT strode into the transporter room, where Lieutenant Kyle was standing behind the controls.

"Scotty," the captain's voice said from the comm, "can you beam all of those people out of there?"

"We're scanning, sir," Kyle muttered.

"We're still scanning, Captain," Scotty called out, "but they're scattered over a lot of territory!" Young Chekov was down there, and Longstreet, and those two had not yet sent out a call to the *Enterprise*. Rachel Zlatopolsky had also gone out with the weeders, as Scotty had started to think of the people in the land vehicles—Rachel, and Emo Tannan, and others from the *Hawking* whom he had come to know before they had beamed down to their new home.

"Can you locate them all?" Captain Kirk asked.

Scotty hurried to Kyle's side. "We're working as hard as we can!" the engineer replied. "For some reason, our sensors aren't working the way they should—it's almost as if something is deflecting the signals."

"Get all of those people out of there, dead or alive," Kirk said.

Scotty looked at the display screen on the transporter control panel. The coordinates of one vehicle—and two people—were displayed, but there was no way to know yet whether those two were alive or dead. Time might be lost bringing up bodies of the dead while those still alive waited for rescue.

"Once I've got precise coordinates for each person," Scotty said, "I'll program the transporter to pluck them up one after another, but it'll take time with this bloody interference." No, he thought; interference was not an accurate term for whatever was confusing the sensors. It was almost as if something below was throwing up a kind of shield.

"Now, Scotty."

"I'm working as we speak, Captain." Scotty's and Kyle's fingers flew over the controls. "We're locked on two people right now. We can get them out if there's nothing in the ground to stop the scan or the transporter beam." He did not want to dwell on the possibility that this alien overgrowth might have a way of deflecting the *Enterprise*'s transporter beams. "We've got a dozen other people besides our two laddies to rescue, don't we?"

"An even dozen," Kirk replied.

"Well, what other kind of dozen can there be," Scotty said softly.

*   *   *

Kirk found himself smiling at Scotty's comment, despite the gravity of their situation. The ability to smile or laugh, even at such an inappropriate moment—it made him wonder about the so-called callousness of professionals in a crisis. They had to step back, and even accept failure, or they would not be able to go on to the next job.

And at the moment, his chief engineer Scotty would be keeping any emotional stresses in check while trying to save whomever he could.

"Scotty?" Kirk asked.

"We have coordinates for six now, Captain," Scotty said.

Kirk felt a moment of uncertainty. Would it be better to beam up those six people now and then get the others? Or wait until all fourteen were found, as Scotty was attempting to do? Three or four people might die waiting for all the coordinates to be set, but if they started beaming some up now . . . better to save a few than to lose them all.

Either plan had the same drawback: lives that could have been saved might slip away during delay.

"Scotty," Kirk said, "can you start beaming people up while you continue your scan?"

"I canna do it at these levels of power, Captain! We're peering right through the crust to make certain we don't miss anyone, and that takes power from the transporter!"

"I agree with Mr. Scott," Spock said from his station.

Kirk's hands tightened into fists. "Scotty, can you use less power for your scan and start beaming up the people you've located?"

"Aye," Scotty's voice replied, "and if you order me to, I will."

Kirk waited for only a moment, and then made his decision.

Chekov had felt his vehicle fall into the rift that had suddenly opened in the ground, then land with an impact that had knocked out the vehicle's lights and had nearly thrown him against his control panel. Either the rift was not as deep as he had feared, or the vehicle had fetched up against a ledge. In the darkness, he could not see what had happened, or even if it was possible for him and Longstreet to get out and climb out of the chasm.

He thought of what he had seen in the crevasse as they fell. A thick green alien substance had been seeping up from the opening in the ground. It was probably still there, preparing to engulf them before it flowed onto the surface.

"Farley," Chekov said, "can you hear me?"

"I'm all right," Longstreet's voice said into his headset.

"Chekov to Cortés." There was no answer. "Chekov to Glakov—can anyone hear me?" He heard only silence in response, and wondered if any of the others had survived.

Chekov reached for his communicator and flipped it open. "Chekov to *Enterprise*," he said. "Come in, *Enterprise*. Longstreet and I are trapped in a rift, and cannot get out."

There was no reply.

"Chekov to *Enterprise*." His communicator hissed at him, as if mocking him.

"Pavel," Longstreet said, "do you hear that sound?"

Chekov strained to hear. The hissing was louder now, and he realized then that this sound was not being emitted by his communicator. It was coming from outside his vehicle, as if something was eating away at the carapace protecting him and Longstreet.

Leander Cortés sat in the darkness, listening to the beating of his heart in the silence, his hand phaser pressed to his chest. He knew now that he would die as soon as he heard—or felt—the intruder biomass inside the carapace. Somehow, the green stuff had still not eaten through to him.

But the telltale hiss was still there, outside, and he knew that it would become louder just before the shielding was eaten away. The carapace would go first, long before the body of the vehicle. There would be a sudden rise in the pitch of the hiss, and the green mass would roll in and smother him.

What am I waiting for, he asked himself. The outcome was certain. Was the *Enterprise* capable of lifting him from this peril, from his death? There was no one to ask; he could only imagine what the *Enterprise* might be able to do on the basis of what he had seen of the vessel's capabilities. They would either dig him out somehow with their phasers, or try to beam him free. But could that be done through all this rock, dirt, and biomass?

Maybe, he thought bleakly, the green mass was impenetrable to the starship's transporter beam. Maybe it could quickly repair any damage the phasers inflicted, making rescue impossible.

It occurred to Cortés then that in the natural course of events he would have died centuries ago, back on Earth.

That was where his bones should have been now, resting across the galaxy in the soil of Earth, rather than waiting to be dissolved in the juices of an amorphous alien enemy that knew nothing of him as an individual.

When he had chosen exile from Earth, knowing that he would never see the world he had known again, he and his comrades had let themselves be drawn into a game not of their choosing—one created long ago, when humanity, in the form of the Federation and its arm, Starfleet, had extended human frontiers beyond the solar system. That he was here, waiting to die, was one small result of that game of interstellar sovereignty. He wondered if it might have happened differently, whether conflict both among human beings and between his kind and aliens was inevitable or necessary. . . .

The hissing sound broke in on his thoughts. This was death, the very end, "the distinguished thing," as one great novelist had said in his last moments of life—the time when you learn everything of what may come, or learn nothing, since there might be nothing left alive with which to learn.

He reached out into the darkness with his gloved hand and felt the strange soft mass moving toward him. His glove began to hiss from the contact with the alien acids. The darkness shimmered before his eyes with an infinity of small explosions, as if a whole universe was coming to an end—

—and when he could see that he was sitting in a lighted room, he knew that the *Enterprise* had plucked him from his death.

* * *

As two sets of arms helped him to his feet in the transporter room, Cortés saw that they belonged to Dr. McCoy and Dr. Soong.

"Dr. McCoy," he gasped as he found his footing, "how many of the others?"

The physician took a deep breath. "How are you feeling?" McCoy asked.

"How many of us did you rescue?" Cortés demanded, looking around the transporter room. Ilsa Soong moved closer to Anthony Tikriti, to scan him with her medical tricorder; Laure Vidor stood just behind them, with Galvin O'Shea and Tabib Hanse. The two *Enterprise* officers, Chekov and Longstreet, stood near the transporter console, but Rachel was not there. Neither was Nasser al-Aswari, nor Xavier Rodriguez.

Cortés clutched at McCoy's arm. "How many?"

"Nine, counting all of you in here," McCoy replied. "Nurse Chapel's on her way to sickbay with the other two."

"What about Emo Tannan—he was in my vehicle."

McCoy glanced toward Lieutenant Commander Scott at the transporter controls.

"I'm sorry," Scott said. "You were the only one who came up from your position. We couldna get a lock on your friend."

Emo was dead, then. Cortés had hoped that somehow he might still be alive, that he had only been knocked unconscious by their vehicle's fall into the crevasse. The green biomass had devoured him. If Emo had died before that thing swallowed him, perhaps it was a mercy.

"And we didn't pick up Rachel," Scott continued in a

somber voice. Cortés closed his eyes for a moment and mourned for the dead, lost so far from home.

"My kinsman Dmitri," he heard Chekov say, "did not make it to safety, either. I found him only to lose him again."

"Captain Cortés," Dr. Soong asked as she scanned him with her medical tricorder, "do you feel any injuries?"

"Yes," he said, knowing how little she and McCoy could do for the kinds of wounds he felt.

"We had better take you to sickbay," McCoy said as he and Soong gently took his arms and led him out of the transporter room.

A dejected Chekov had reported to Kirk that his kinsman Dmitri Glakov was among the lost. Now the ensign was back at his station, sitting to the right of Sulu. The Russian had asked to remain on duty, as Kirk had known he would. Perhaps Chekov was thinking of how the older man might have died on Earth had he not left in the *Hawking,* and might never have been known to his descendant at all except as a distant figure of family legend.

Longstreet was on duty at the communications station. The image of Teressa Aliss was on the screen. Kirk saw that she was sitting in some sort of land vehicle, with her aide Ojuremi at her side and Uhura in the seat behind them. They had gone to the western edge of the city, Uhura had reported to him earlier, to wait for New Ibadan's defenders to return and be there to help if necessary.

"Thank you, Captain," the Meropean woman said, "for rescuing . . . our fighters. I am only sorry that you couldn't save all of those brave people—it's a great loss to us."

As Kirk stood up at his command station, he noted that the First Citizen now spoke of the people from the *Hawking* as she would of her own citizens. He only wished that this acceptance could have come about under happier circumstances.

"But now, Captain Kirk," she continued, "the attacker is at our gates, and we are powerless to stop it. We're evacuating the entire riverfront and telling everyone on the edges of the city to leave their houses and head toward the city center. We can't stop this invader. Order is being maintained for now, but soon people will begin to panic." She paused and stared at him from the viewscreen, expecting perhaps that he would tell her that there was not much that could be done.

"Mr. Spock," Kirk said firmly, "we are going to have to stop this biomass now and find out more about what kind of life-form it may be later." He did not turn around to look at his friend.

"I agree, Captain," he heard the Vulcan say. "My advice is that we now follow the same procedure as Captain Cortés and his comrades did, but using the *Enterprise*'s phasers—at their lowest power first, on stun, and then on maximum. We can sweep the area around New Ibadan in a matter of minutes."

Teressa Aliss was silent. "Did you hear that?" Kirk asked after a few moments.

"Yes," she said.

"And do you agree?"

She nodded. "We have no choice. Give your order, Captain Kirk."

He sat down at his station. "Prepare to fire ship's phasers," he said in a loud voice. The face of Teressa Aliss faded from the bridge viewscreen and was replaced by an image of Merope IV.

"Phasers ready," Sulu said from his forward station.

"Mr. Sulu," Kirk said, "prepare to sweep the area just in front of the advancing biomass."

"Aye, aye, sir," Sulu said. "Setting automatic firing co-ordinates now."

"Fire!" Kirk said.

Chapter Eleven

AS TERESSA WATCHED the western horizon from the outskirts of New Ibadan, the massive phaser beam reached down from the sky and plowed the ground in front of the green invader, throwing up geysers of dirt and rock. A roar assaulted her ears, followed by a high-pitched whine.

As the phaser went north to cut its path of destruction around the city, Teressa saw first-hand what terrifying power was contained in a starship—for good or evil. But what if the difference between good and evil was not always clear? Was some kind of mistake being made here? This was an alien world, where human beings had colonized only part of one continent. The settlers had been here for only forty years, with large portions of New Niger still unsettled and the other two continents still partly unsurveyed. There was too much that remained unknown to the colonists about this planet. To strike at the green mass might prove to be a grave error.

No, she told herself, and she thought about how the green wall could overwhelm New Ibadan. Everything they had built here would be dissolved by the acids; people would die by the thousands if the growth was not stopped. James Kirk and his *Enterprise* could not possibly rescue all of the Meropeans, or even a small percentage of them.

The phaser raged off to her right. She turned around and walked back to her land vehicle, where Trent Ojuremi and Lieutenant Uhura sat waiting for her. She had noticed signs of tension and wariness in both of them when Uhura had beamed down to New Ibadan, but they seemed to have put aside their differences in the face of the alien threat. All three of them had soon been busy conferring with the city council and the leaders of the civic patrols on ways to keep the citizens of New Ibadan calm.

Teressa saw the look of awe on her aide's face as she climbed into the cab beside him.

"Frightening," Trent said over the roar that was still penetrating the closed cab.

Teressa sighed as dust pelted the vehicle's transparent windshield. "Leander Cortés and his comrades couldn't stop that biomass even with their mounted phasers set to disruption. Using a starship's phasers on stun against it may only provoke the growth to more destructive efforts in its own defense."

"Teressa." Trent shook his head. "I've never heard you sound so defeatist. You also continue to assume that some sort of intelligence is controlling that . . . that moss patch."

"We don't know anything about this growth." She

thought of the dreams that had plagued her and so many others, of her growing conviction that they were facing some sort of alien mind.

He leaned toward her. "Messanga Watson sent a message just before the *Enterprise* opened up with phaser fire. He says that Shaku is secure for now, although he's spotted a wall of the green stuff some miles away from the town. He's ordered everyone in Shaku to be prepared to flee at a moment's notice."

Teressa nodded absently. The people of Shiroro and Gombé in the east were evacuating to the Kainji Mountains, while those of Jalinga and Bakundi were heading downriver, away from the green growth. That might protect the inhabitants of those towns and settlements for a while, but once New Ibadan was swallowed, the growth might appear in even more regions and surround any refuge that other people had found.

No, she thought. No matter how bad it looked, she would not acknowledge defeat until she was forced to do so.

"We should contact Captain Kirk," Uhura said, "and find out what the ship's sensor scans are showing."

Teressa reached forward and touched a small panel on the vehicle's console. Kirk's face appeared on the comm's small screen. "Kirk here," the captain said.

"Captain Kirk, is the phaser beam having any effect at all?" she asked.

"No," Kirk replied. Teressa felt Trent tense beside her. "Running the beam in front of the mat has not made it retreat. We will have to disrupt it—at least its leading edge."

Trent leaned back in his seat. "Will that be any more effective?" Teressa said.

"There's no way anything can withstand phaser disruption," James Kirk replied. "Mr. Spock assures me that the mat would have to be made of solid neutronium to do so, and that would make the biomass so heavy that it would sink through the planet. No, this has to be a biological organism. Rest assured that it will be . . . mowed."

She heard Captain Kirk chuckle mirthlessly. "What's so funny?" she said.

"You have a very big yard."

Uhura and Trent chuckled, but Teressa knew from the sound that their laughter was only an involuntary release of tension. She smiled in spite of herself. "This is no time for humor, Captain."

"Quite right, Ms. Aliss." His expression grew serious. "Still no signs of retreat in the mat."

"Captain," Scotty's voice called out from engineering, "we're using power at an incredible rate! We canna keep this up for much longer!"

Kirk tensed at his bridge command station. "I'm aware of that, Mr. Scott, but there should be enough power for the time we've set. We can recharge after that."

As he looked at the bridge viewscreen, the first program of phaser fire ended. "Mr. Sulu," he said, "prepare to fire directly into the mat. Move phaser fire in the same sweep around the city—only the edge."

"Yes, sir," Sulu said.

Kirk stood up and stared at the screen, where magnification now showed a vertical view of the Meropean city, with its surrounding green assailant still closing in, leaving him no further choices to make. The biomass now covered the waterfront and the houses near it and was advancing north toward Yakuru Plaza, while from the east, the thick green stuff was now less than two kilometers from the terrace where the reception had been held for the people from the *Hawking*. No escape was possible for the people trapped inside New Ibadan, most of whom were now retreating toward the center of the city and the areas around the plaza and the terrace.

"Fire directly at the leading edge of the mat," Kirk said, "same pattern."

"Aye, aye, Captain," Sulu said.

Kirk stood up and watched the beam pierce the atmosphere and then begin its deadly work on the city's encircling attacker.

And suddenly he was thrown backward. He fell against his command station chair and onto the floor, writhing from the pain that tore into his head. The blow had hit him with a low thud in his ears, knocking him over, and now the sound of beating continued, like the pounding of some massive alien heart.

Somehow he managed to turn his head and saw that Chekov and Sulu were also down, knocked out of their seats. Chekov's body twisted from side to side; Sulu grabbed at his own head with clawlike fingers. Behind him, Kirk heard Longstreet groan loudly, as though he were badly wounded.

"Spock!" he cried out—but there was no reply.

* * *

A giant invisible fist struck Scotty, hurling him into a panel of engineering controls. He clutched at the control panel, then slid to the floor as the fist continued to pummel him.

Lieutenant Darmer lay next to him; the young engineer seemed to be unconscious. The rest of the engineering crew on duty had been strewn across the floor like a set of discarded dolls. An alarm started to sound, quickly rising in pitch.

The *Enterprise* was under attack, Scotty realized, but who or what was the attacker? The weedy Meropean biomass? As soon as that thought came to him, a fiery pain ripped at his innards and rippled up his spine.

The phasers were already being drained of their power. The ship's engines might not be able to withstand whatever force was being directed against them.

"My engines," Scotty mumbled, "my poor bairns," and then a spasm convulsed him.

The force of the blow threw McCoy across sickbay and into a diagnostic panel above one of the beds. He crashed to the floor as someone screamed.

"Doctor," a woman's voice called out, "Dr. McCoy." He recognized the voice of Christine Chapel, but could not see where the nurse was. Laure Vidor, who had come to sickbay with Cortés and his other surviving comrades, clawed at the floor as if intent on digging her way through the *Enterprise*. Another woman lay near Laure, writhing in a seizure, her long dark hair spread over the floor; that was Ilsa Soong.

A part of McCoy's mind was coiled up inside him, trying to shield itself from the pain. It was almost as though his entire nervous system was suffering from short circuiting, or some kind of overload. The pain went on pounding him, throbbing at his temples, beating against his chest.

McCoy tried to make himself lie still, but his arms and legs refused to obey him, flailing against the floor until he was afraid his bones might break. He waited, enduring the blows, until the trembling was past, then felt himself shiver.

The atmosphere around him felt cold, as if the ship's life-support systems were failing. Shock, he thought, I'm going into shock now, and he wondered if there was anyone left alive in sickbay to help him.

"Spock," Kirk muttered, "Spock." He tried to get up, to crawl aft toward Spock's station, but as he rose on all fours the hammer blows again shook his entire body. He fell forward on his face and lay still, and that seemed to help the pain.

After a few moments, he tried to rise again, but the pain gripped his very will. He lay there, unable to move . . . after what seemed at least an hour, Kirk managed to move his head. At last he rolled over on his back, and found Spock's face looking down at him.

"Spock," Kirk gasped, "what's going on?"

"I am not certain," Spock said, "but I have a few suppositions." He grasped Kirk by the shoulders and eased him into a sitting position. On the floor, near the communications station, Farley Longstreet looked dazed, but he was sitting up, gingerly flexing his arms; he seemed to be recovering.

"My God," Sulu muttered. The helmsman was on the floor; he rolled to one side and rubbed at the back of his neck. "What was that?"

"I believe," Spock replied, "that when we actually began to disrupt the substance of the Meropean biomass, a neural net struck back at us by sending a pulse at us, perhaps through our own phaser beam. I managed to turn the beam off manually, and that was the moment when the attack seemed to subside. Are you recovering now, Captain?"

Kirk allowed Spock to prop his shoulders against the edge of his command chair's seat. "I think so." His hands felt cold, but some warmth was returning to his arms. He rubbed his hands together as Spock moved aft, murmured a few words to Longstreet, then sat down at the communications station.

"Bridge to engineering," Spock said.

"Scott here," the chief engineer's voice said a few moments later. "Can you hear me, Captain?"

"Spock here," the Vulcan replied. "We hear you, Mr. Scott."

"What's going on?" Scotty said. "We've lost power, our engines apparently aren't functioning, and our firepower's gone. Ivan Darmer's down with a broken arm, and Yeoman Padma's unconscious and bleeding from the scalp—she may have a serious head injury. I've been calling to sickbay for help, but there's no answer."

"Bridge to sickbay," Spock said. "Dr. McCoy, can you hear me?"

"Spock?" Kirk was relieved to hear McCoy's voice. "We're getting calls from all over the ship," the physician continued. "We haven't been able to answer them all—sounds like every deck was affected. I've been telling the injured to get here on foot if they can. We'll get medical personnel to those who aren't ambulatory as soon as we're able to walk. What the hell's going on?"

"I will inform you of that," Spock said, "as soon as I have had more time to consider and analyze these events. How many injured are in sickbay now?"

"None, fortunately. We're all shaken up, but everybody here seems to be in fairly sound condition. Gave myself and Nurse Chapel a quick scan, and we're both showing the aftereffects of shock."

Spock glanced back at Kirk. "All personnel on the bridge also seem to be recovering," the Vulcan said, "so I will now leave you to your medical duties, Doctor. Spock out."

Spock got up from the communications station, helped Lieutenant Longstreet to his feet and eased him into his chair, then went to his own station. "Think I'm all right," Longstreet said, "but I've got the worst headache of my life."

"The entire ship has been affected," Spock said from his computer station, "as have, it seems, all our personnel."

"How about you?" Kirk asked.

Spock turned toward him. "My mental disciplines enabled me to block the attack as soon as it commenced. If I had waited a few moments longer, I would not have been able to do so."

Kirk's head still throbbed, and his vision was slightly blurred. He looked around the bridge, and saw that Sulu and Chekov were now sitting up, looking almost normal. "But why did it attack us now, and not sooner?" Kirk asked.

"I surmise that the biomass—the life-form—would not respond," Spock answered, "until its actual body was attacked in some significant way."

"In other words, until we attacked it wholesale." Kirk slowly got to his feet, but his legs shook so badly that he was forced to sit down abruptly at his command station. "So is this thing intelligent?"

"That is difficult to say conclusively, Captain. It may not have centers of self-consciousness as we do, but it may have an accumulation of survival data of some complexity, data that would enable it to respond in virtuoso fashion while still not being a conscious intelligence as we understand one to be."

"Mr. Spock," Sulu asked, "do you think the earlier uneasiness we felt near that Meropean settlement, just before that chasm opened up, might have been a warning of some kind?"

"It might very well have been," Spock said.

"What other damage have we sustained?" Kirk asked.

"There are no reports of any deaths aboard ship," Spock said, "but our main computer seems to be in a kind of shock and reacting very slowly to my commands. Both our warp drive and our impulse engines are no longer functioning, and neither are our defensive shields nor our weapons, according to my readings."

"I can confirm that for you, Mr. Spock," Scotty's voice cut in. "We canna get away, nor can we defend ourselves."

Kirk sighed. His head still hurt, but his vision was clearing. "Did we at least stop the advance of the biomass on New Ibadan?"

"Unknown," Spock said, "until our sensors are again functioning and we are able to communicate with Teressa Aliss."

"Uhura to *Enterprise*," Uhura said into her communicator, "come in, *Enterprise*." She had been calling for several minutes now, and there was still no reply. Either her signal was being blocked somehow, or something had gone seriously wrong aboard ship.

"The growth seems to have stopped," Trent said from the seat in front of her, "when the phaser beam shut down."

"I think so, too," Teressa Aliss said next to him.

Uhura rested her arms on the back of the seat in front of her and stared through the vehicle's windshield at the green mat, now scarcely a kilometer away from the western limits of the city. She felt a great uneasiness that might easily turn into terror. What else was that alien thing readying to send against the Meropeans? The wall might simply start moving—growing—again, and that would be threatening enough.

"Still no word from the *Enterprise*," Trent muttered. "That worries me. I hope nothing's happened to the starship."

"I don't think anything could have happened to the ship," Uhura said, but she was no longer so certain of that. Without the *Enterprise*, this world would be helpless. She was trying to keep herself calm and composed, not wanting to provoke Trent or the First Citizen into panic, but inwardly she despaired. How could this have happened to a thriving colony? Why had this threat not been foreseen, or uncovered by the first settlers? Why had the mossy green mat, and whatever might be controlling it, left these people alone until now?

"The wind is increasing," Trent said, leaning forward to gaze through the windshield.

She saw that the wind was picking up rapidly; soon small rocks and pebbles were pelting their windshield. The wind howled as loose tree limbs and more rocks swept past them. Uhura peered at the mat ahead; it had not moved.

The wind would be at gale force soon. "We have to get out of here," Teressa Aliss said to Trent, "while we still can."

"I'll drive us back manually." Trent took the controls and began to back up. Uhura was suddenly pushed against her seat as the rear end of the vehicle dropped.

Trent looked back. "A crack!" he cried out. "The ground's opening up behind us!"

The vehicle was beginning to slide. Trent raced the engine, but Uhura knew that it was too late; there was no surface behind them. The vehicle slid backward, at a slight angle, scraping against the walls of the crevasse that had appeared at their left and right.

"We're trapped!" Trent shouted. "We should have left earlier!"

"Stop it," Teressa said. The other woman pressed her hand against the control panel to open the comm. "Aliss to *Enterprise*, Aliss to *Enterprise*, can you hear me?"

There was no response. Trent was right, Uhura thought; something had happened to the starship.

"Aliss to *Enterprise*," the First Citizen repeated.

"Uhura to *Enterprise*," Uhura said into her communicator, but she no longer expected any answer from the captain.

Trent said, "We'll never get out of here."

"We will."

"That thing's going to swallow us up."

Uhura heard Teressa mutter a few words that might have been a curse. "Not if I can help it," the other woman said softly. "Aliss to *Enterprise*."

"Enterprise," a man's voice replied, but the wind above the crevasse shrieked so loudly that Uhura could barely hear him. "Kirk here." The captain's face, streaked by lines of static, appeared on the control panel's small screen.

"Captain," Teressa said, "Trent and Uhura and I are trapped in a crevasse—it's the same thing that happened to Cortés and his people. Can you beam us out?"

"Not right now," Kirk replied. "Our ship's computer has been damaged—we're already working on repairs. We'll get to you as soon as we can."

"We'd be most grateful if you would," the First Citizen said.

"Kirk out." The captain's face winked out.

The vehicle slid down another meter, then seemed to lodge itself against the walls of the crevasse. They might be safe for a while, Uhura told herself, as long as they did not slip down any deeper.

Trent turned around to gaze in her direction. He

seemed embarrassed by his earlier show of fear. "Are you all right?" Uhura asked.

He nodded, but did not look directly at her.

"The *Enterprise* will beam us out of here in a few moments," Uhura said, trying to sound reassuring. She thought of all the people waiting in the central areas of New Ibadan for their leader, probably wondering what had happened to her.

"We have to get out of here," Teressa said, "and I'm not about to abandon my people. If the captain can beam us aboard his ship, he can also beam me back to my city. I'll stand with my people and fight for as long as possible."

"We shouldn't have come out here," Trent said.

Teressa turned toward him. "I needed to see for myself exactly what we're up against."

"I know that, but we didn't need to see it at such close range."

"We had to find out what we could," Uhura said, "and be here in case—"

"We knew what we needed to know," Trent interrupted. "The Starfleet personnel who first scanned and explored this planet didn't do a very good job, did they?" He turned away from Uhura. "We had no warning of what would come—that our entire colony would be at risk."

"Enough," the Meropean woman said. "Ever since the arrival of the *Enterprise,* you've been complaining. You act as if we're somehow diminished by Starfleet's help. What exactly is the problem?"

Trent did not reply. Uhura was about to speak, but thought better of it.

The vehicle shifted a bit. Uhura tensed, but the movement stopped. They did not seem about to descend further into the opening, but she was afraid to move, afraid that even the slightest movement might send them plummeting into the abyss.

"I don't know," Trent said, looking around nervously, "but somehow I get the feeling that the *Enterprise* and the *Hawking* and the new colonists helped to wake up this thing."

"Oh, come on, Trent." Teressa frowned. "It destroyed that settlement near Shaku well before our visitors arrived. The presence of the *Enterprise* couldn't have caused that."

"But things got a lot worse after that, after the starship—"

"Trent, the thing was here, and sooner or later we would have had to face it."

"It hates us," he said. "I know that sounds irrational, but I feel it."

"It's not irrational at all," Uhura murmured. "I feel it, too, almost as if something outside of me is trying—"

"Kirk to Aliss," a voice said as the small comm screen lit up once more.

"We're still here, Captain," Teressa said.

Kirk's image appeared on the screen. "I have some bad news for all of you." Uhura had already noticed the dismay on his face. "Our computer is malfunctioning. Our power systems and our transporter won't function properly until we get the computer up and running again. Can you three hold out for a while?"

Teressa nodded. "I think so. We're all right at the moment, but it may not be long before that growth moves in on this crevasse."

"Is it moving now?" Kirk asked.

"I'm fairly sure it isn't. I haven't seen any signs of that, anyway, but—"

"Hang on, Ms. Aliss. I'm going to give an order for a shuttlecraft to come and pick you up if necessary."

"But we can't climb out of here," Trent said, with an edge of fear in his voice.

"The rescuers can bring a cable to lift you and your vehicle out of the chasm," Kirk said.

"But they may get here too late," Trent said more sharply.

"Is the biomass moving?" Kirk asked.

"I don't think so, Captain," Uhura said. "But since we're below ground, we may not see the mass coming at us until it's too late."

"I understand," the captain said. "Scotty, how is work going on the transporter?" Uhura could not hear an answer from the chief engineer. "Very well," Kirk continued. "Sulu and Chekov, go to the shuttlebay. If the transporter isn't on line by the time you get there, you'll head for the surface in a shuttlecraft and get those three people down there out of danger."

"Captain," Teressa murmured, "I have more to say." She looked toward Trent. "We may not get out of this. You have some obligation to Lieutenant Uhura, but don't let your people take unreasonable risks trying to save Trent and me. Regardless of what happens to us, do what you can for our people, even if it's to evacuate them to another world. I'm guessing that the smaller settlements outside New Ibadan are safe for now, and if the mat has stopped moving temporarily, the people in the city may be able to hold out for a while."

"I've already sent a subspace message to Starfleet," Kirk said, "saying that we may have to evacuate Merope Four, but it will take days for other starships to get here, maybe longer."

"I know that. Just do what's possible."

"Hang on, Teressa," Kirk said. "Uhura, get on the comm if anything changes. Kirk out."

"We're not getting out of here, are we?" Trent asked.

Uhura leaned forward. "I'll be honest with you both," she said. "I think that, without the transporter, our chances are pretty slim. The shuttlecraft will take longer to reach us. About all we can do is hope that we and our vehicle don't fall another centimeter deeper and that the wind dies down enough to allow the *Enterprise* rescue party to land."

"So we're going to die," he said.

"Don't count us out until we're out," Teressa said.

"There's something I never told you, Teressa. It doesn't much matter if I tell you now. Uhura knows much of this, but there are some things I never had a chance to tell her, either." Trent was silent for a few moments. "I wanted to serve with Starfleet once. It was my dream all through childhood. I was in love with Uhura, and we wanted to be Starfleet officers together."

"Trent," Uhura whispered, thinking of what might have been.

"Uhura and I both applied to Starfleet Academy. They accepted her, but I was turned down. I was stunned, I couldn't understand it—I knew I had every qualification they could have wanted. I hated them for rejecting me, and then I started to hate Uhura because she chose the Academy instead of me. I went there to see her later on, I asked her to resign and come away with me, but she refused. That was the last time I saw her, until the *Enterprise* came here."

Teressa was silent.

"You might have enlisted after the Academy turned you down," Uhura said gently. "I sometimes wondered why you didn't. You wouldn't have been the first crewmember to rise to an officer's position from the ranks."

"Oh, but enlisting wasn't good enough for Trent Ojuremi." She heard bitterness and self-mockery in his voice. "If they didn't want to train me as an officer, I certainly wasn't going to consign myself to being a humble yeoman. I also didn't want to take the chance that Starfleet might reject me again—that would have been an even more unbearable humiliation. So I spent the next few years doing my best to drown my sorrows and make a mess of my life. In other words, I demonstrated that Starfleet was right to reject my application."

"Trent," she murmured.

"I couldn't have admitted that before now, even to myself, but it's the truth. I see it now. If an old friend hadn't found me on the street and practically forced me to enroll at his university, I might still be pursuing my self-destructive course. And now I wonder if I came to Merope Four to get a fresh start or only because I thought that I might have a bit more status among the colonists here than I would have had on Earth."

"You've done a lot for us," Teressa said to her aide. "You've worked hard, you have been my right hand, you've given us the beginnings of a university."

"All of which might have been for nothing."

"No, Trent," the Meropean woman said. "I won't accept that until there's no choice."

Uhura was about to speak when the vehicle shifted again. She froze, expecting it to drop, to fall so deep into the crevasse that rescue would be impossible.

"Comrades," Uhura said then, "we'd better not wait for rescuers. I think we should start figuring out how we're going to get out of this predicament by ourselves."

Chapter Twelve

As HIKARU SULU brought the shuttlecraft *Columbus* through the storm clouds over the plain, a flash of white lightning stabbed down into the green mat that surrounded New Ibadan. A moment later he was startled by a second jab, which illuminated the green attacker. To the starboard side of the shuttlecraft, Sulu saw that a thick bridge of biomass, at least two kilometers wide, had grown across the Temba River to the southern waterfront of the city. The growth seemed to have halted for now, but on either side of the bridge, the river had begun to rise.

The water might flood parts of the city; he was surprised that small inlets hadn't already begun to form along the banks. Maybe the green stuff was absorbing most of the water. Commander Spock would be able to find out, now that the *Enterprise*'s sensors were working again.

When a third flash of lightning died, there was still enough daylight to see by, and Sulu noticed that the thick green mat of alien foliage extended as far as his eyes could see, well beyond the horizon presented by the shuttlecraft's altitude. All they could hope for now, he realized, was that the stuff stopped growing and flowing long enough for more starships to get here and evacuate the colonists.

"It looks hopeless," Ensign Chekov said at his right, "and Mr. Spock says that there is even more of the growth coming up from the crust of the planet."

Sulu listened absently as he scanned for the land vehicle that was trapped in the crevasse that had opened up west of the city. He had a fix on it now, then let out his breath in disappointment when he saw the readings. The vehicle had fallen so far into the crevasse that he doubted anyone could have survived the fall.

"I've found the vehicle," Sulu said, "and it looks bad. It's fallen to the bottom of that rift."

Chekov leaned forward. "Shuttlecraft *Columbus* to *Enterprise*," the Russian said into the comm.

"Spock here," the first officer's voice replied.

"We have located the land vehicle," Chekov said.

"It's at the bottom of the fissure below us," Sulu added. "Frankly, it doesn't look good. Advise now—can you beam them out, or should we go in and attempt a rescue?"

"Transporter operation is still uncertain," Spock said. "Proceed with rescue using the shuttlecraft. Spock out."

"Shuttlecraft *Columbus* to Teressa Aliss," Chekov said.

"First Citizen, do you read? Respond if you hear us. *Columbus* to Aliss, can you hear me?" He let out his breath. "*Columbus* to Uhura, *Columbus* to Uhura, come in, Uhura."

"I'll keep looking," Sulu muttered, but he was already losing hope.

Uhura had been clinging to the wall of dirt and rock, digging in with her hands and the toes of her booted feet, when the ground shifted. She had nearly lost her grip; she had looked down just in time to see the vehicle two meters below her drop into the darkness.

She hung on to the rope that bound her to Trent and Teressa, telling herself again not to look down. Lifting her head slightly, she saw that Trent had nearly reached the top of the ridge, with Teressa just below him.

He had tied the rope to her. He had insisted that they get out of the vehicle and try to climb out of the crevasse just before she was about to propose the same course of action. She thought of how slowly and painstakingly he had opened the door on his side of the vehicle, so as not to jar the craft. He might still be just as afraid as he had sounded when they had been sitting in the vehicle waiting for rescue, but he was doing an excellent job of hiding whatever fears he felt.

Ignoring the pain in her shoulders, Uhura reached up with her right hand, felt another of the indentations Trent had dug out with his hands and feet, and pulled herself up. Her feet rested on a ledge as she pressed herself against the wall. Where would they go if they did get out?

Back to the city? Would they even be able to make it there on foot, with the biomass probably blocking their way and the ground opening into fissures?

She pulled herself up, felt her hands slip, and suddenly found herself swinging away from the wall. She hung there, dangling from the rope around her waist.

"Trent!" she cried out. "Trent!" She swung toward the wall again and grabbed at what looked like a ledge. Her fingers dug into the dirt; she held on, afraid to move.

"Uhura!" Trent's voice seemed far away. "Are you all right?"

"Just fine," she gasped. The pain in her shoulders was worse.

"The rope's too taut," she heard him say. "I can't move until you get farther up and closer to me. You've got to climb up some more."

"We'll make it," she whispered, and forced herself to climb.

"Do you read me?" Sulu said.

"Look over there!" Chekov called out.

Sulu saw someone now, to his west, a small figure standing near the crevasse. He piloted the shuttlecraft in that direction; the view of the plain on his small screen pulled in to reveal that the figure was that of Trent Ojuremi. A rope was around the man's waist, and now Sulu saw that Ojuremi was trying to pull someone else out of the fissure who was attached to his rope.

The shuttlecraft dropped down and landed about two hundred meters away as a dark figure with short whitish hair crawled over the edge of the chasm and collapsed next to Ojuremi, followed by another familiar form in a Starfleet uniform.

"*Columbus* to *Enterprise,* Chekov here," Chekov said. Sulu breathed a sigh of relief at the sight of his fellow officer and her companions. "We have located Uhura, Aliss, and Ojuremi. Somehow they got out of their vehicle and climbed out of the fissure—they're safe, and seem uninjured."

"*Enterprise* to *Columbus,*" the captain said, "Kirk here. I'm very glad to hear it."

"We've landed," Sulu said. "Should we pick them up and return to the *Enterprise?*"

"Get them aboard your craft first," Captain Kirk replied. "Aliss and Ojuremi may want to go back to their city, to be with their people."

"Would that be safe?" Chekov asked.

"Our sensors tell us that the biomass is still growing," Kirk said, "and more fissures are opening up around New Ibadan, but the mass is now moving toward the city more slowly. Let's hope that gives us enough time to evacuate the population. I advise you to get Uhura and the others aboard the shuttlecraft quickly, and then head toward the city if that's where the First Citizen decides to go. At the moment, you'd all be safer even there than staying where you are."

"Aye, aye, sir," Sulu said.

"I mean it, Sulu," Kirk went on. "You're safer in the air than on the ground there, so don't wait there any longer than you have to."

"I will go get them," Chekov said as he got up, opened the shuttlecraft exit, and went outside. Aliss and Ojuremi were already stumbling toward the shuttlecraft, led by Uhura; the three stopped for a moment to untie the rope that still linked them. Sulu felt the floor of his vehicle tremble under his feet. Before he could wonder at what had caused the shaking, the shuttlecraft shook again, nearly throwing him from his seat.

Sulu had a sudden impulse to get out of the craft. Outside, Chekov hurried toward Uhura and her companions. The First Citizen was frantically waving her arms at Chekov, as if trying to warn him of some danger. She halted, stared in the direction of the shuttlecraft, then waved an arm toward Sulu. Chekov beckoned to her and the others; now Uhura shook her head at him and pointed at Sulu and the shuttlecraft. The Russian quickly turned around and then pulled his communicator from his belt.

"Hikaru, get out now!" Chekov's voice said from the comm. Even as Sulu heard the last word of the ensign's warning, he felt the craft falling. The shuttlecraft's nose went forward, throwing him against the control panel. The lights flickered; the craft bounced violently to a stop. In the few moments of light, Sulu saw that his forward view was now a wall of rock and dirt.

There was no way he could take off, as far as he could see. The shuttlecraft's exit was still open, but the wall just outside it was too close for any escape to be possible. Sulu crept back toward the controls, pressed a panel, and heard the craft's door scrape loudly against the wall as it slid shut.

"Sulu to *Enterprise*," he said into the comm, "Sulu to *Enterprise*. Chekov is on the surface with the others, but

I'm still inside the *Columbus,* trapped in a fissure that suddenly opened up under my craft."

"Mr. Sulu," a voice said, "Spock here."

"Can you beam me out of here?"

"Negative," the Vulcan's voice replied. "Mr. Scott informs me that the computer will not follow orders to activate the transporter."

"We have your location, Lieutenant Sulu," Kirk's voice cut in. "What's your status?"

"No injuries," Sulu replied, "and the exit is closed. Life-support systems are still functioning. I'm in fairly good shape, Captain, but I'm not doing anyone any good here."

He looked around, wondering if there were some way to get out and climb to the surface, as Uhura and the two Meropeans had managed to do. His safest course of action might be to stay here; the shuttlecraft had provisions aboard, so it should be possible to wait out the time until the transporter was working again. But he might be needed on the surface; he did not know what perils Pavel Chekov and Uhura and the two Meropeans might be facing now. There was also a chance that the fissure that had caught him and his craft might close up again. He wondered if the walls of the chasm could crush the vehicle flat.

"Should I try to get to the surface?" Sulu continued. "Should I climb out?"

"Negative," Kirk replied. "Abandoning the shuttlecraft out there would leave you and the others at the mercy of that biomass. Stay where you are for now."

* * *

Chekov watched as the *Columbus* disappeared into the rift that had suddenly opened. The ground shook under his feet, throwing him against Trent Ojuremi, and for a moment he feared that another chasm would open up and swallow him.

Ojuremi gripped Chekov by the arm. "I tried to warn him," Teressa Aliss said.

"I know," Chekov said.

"We're powerless before this growth, these quakes," Ojuremi went on. "This biomass will keep moving and dissolve New Ibadan. We're helpless."

Chekov heard the distress in the man's voice and saw the fright in Aliss's staring hazel eyes. The effort they must have endured climbing out of the crevasse, the shock of realizing that they were still alive, their fear for their people and their city—all of that, Chekov knew, was enough to affect anyone badly.

Uhura put a hand on Ojuremi's arm. "Trent," she said in a steady voice, "we're safe for the moment. We're not helpless—not yet."

Chekov was still holding his communicator. "Chekov to Sulu," he murmured, "Chekov to Sulu, come in, Sulu," but there was no reply. The shuttlecraft's communications equipment might have been damaged by the fall. Irrationally, Chekov wondered if the biomass had a way of interfering with his communicator; he pushed that thought aside.

He put his communicator back on his belt. "Mr. Chekov," Teressa Aliss said, moving closer to him, "it was one of your kinsmen who was lost defending our city, wasn't it? Captain Cortés told me his story. Dmitri Glakov, I believe his name was."

Chekov nodded. "Yes, he was my kinsman." The woman was obviously attentive to even the smallest of details, but as the leader of a colony, she would have to be.

"He went out to fight for us." Aliss averted her eyes. "I had my doubts about accepting those people from the *Hawking* in our communities. How foolish of me."

"Let's consider what we can do now," Uhura said, "to help Sulu."

Chekov looked toward the fissure into which the *Columbus* had fallen, and wondered if there was any way to get to it and rescue Sulu, who might have been injured. But he held himself back; climbing down into the rift after the shuttlecraft would be dangerous, if not foolhardy.

He took a deep breath, letting his training take control of his impulses, and tried to think. The malevolence of the encroaching green wall, only a kilometer and a half away from him, seemed to be much more than a natural disaster. The green thing that had come out of the planet had a perfect means of self-preservation: absorb all enemies and make them a part of yourself.

Chekov reminded himself that all life was vampiric toward other life, that all biology came out of a cauldron of bloody competition, and that only lately, with what the jungle might say was a growing cowardice, had intelligent life begun to worry about what it ate or destroyed. But even as his thoughtfulness steadied his nerves, it did not remove the possibility that he might be eaten by the vast green growth. Chekov thought of his kinsman

Dmitri, who had met his death in this world, devoured by an alien he could never have imagined.

"We should wait here," Chekov heard Uhura say to the two Meropeans. "The crew of the *Enterprise* will be working to get a fix on us and beam us up, and with any luck, they'll pluck Lieutenant Sulu out of the shuttlecraft."

The ground trembled again, but the four remained on their feet. "We should be with our people," Aliss said. "They may need us, if only for moral support while they wait. . . ." She paused. "Starfleet will probably have to evacuate us, assuming that's even possible."

"The captain has sent out a distress call for other Starfleet vessels," Chekov admitted.

"We have to get back to the city," Ojuremi said. "We've got feet. We can walk back."

Teressa Aliss grabbed her aide's wrist and held it. "Don't be a fool, Trent. More fissures could trap us at any time. We'd better listen to Lieutenant Uhura."

"She is right," Chekov added. "We should stay here."

"For how long?" Ojuremi demanded.

Chekov turned to face the man. "For as long as it takes, until the *Enterprise* picks us up."

"And what if they can't?" Ojuremi asked.

Before Chekov could answer him, the green wall began to glow, and it seemed to him then that the mass would surge forward and quickly close the kilometer between them. He waited, but after a moment of observation, he realized that the wall had not moved.

Suddenly a giant figure stepped out of the green and came slowly forward. Chekov looked up and saw a mammoth simulacrum of Captain Kirk. It had to be a simulacrum, Chekov told himself; it could not possibly be real. The giant Kirk's feet shook the ground; the wind picked up, gusting past Chekov and his companions.

"Do you see that, Uhura?" Chekov asked.

"Yes, I do," the lieutenant replied.

"I see it," Aliss said.

"So do I," Ojuremi added, his voice rising to a higher pitch. "What can it be?"

"It cannot be real," Chekov shouted above the rising wind. He pulled out his communicator. "Chekov to *Enterprise*. Four to beam up. Can you get us out of here?" There was no answer. "Chekov to *Enterprise*. Four to beam up. Five if you count Mr. Sulu—he's still trapped in the rift."

The giant image was still walking toward them. Ojuremi let out a cry as the colossal Kirk walked through them as if made of air. Aliss and Uhura looked up at the figure with more astonishment than fear, or so it seemed to Chekov.

The ground shook again, throwing Chekov forward. He held on to his communicator. Aliss lay beside him; as he got up and helped her to her feet, Ojuremi cried out again. The narrow fissure into which the *Columbus* had fallen was yawning, growing wider, and then the shuttlecraft shot out of the ground. Chekov knew at once that the suddenly widening crevasse had pointed the craft upward, giving Sulu the chance he needed to lift free.

"He's out!" Uhura cried.

"Sulu has escaped!" Chekov shouted. The shuttlecraft circled above them, swooping lower and then rising, and

Chekov realized that the same problem still awaited Sulu. If he landed, the ground might open up again to swallow the *Columbus*. This entire planet had turned against the human life-forms that had come here; the alien green biomass was determined to get them.

"Chekov to *Enterprise*," he said into his communicator, "you had better beam us all up now. Sulu's free, he is out of the rift, but he cannot land near us."

"Kirk here," the captain's voice replied. "Transporter's still out—we can't pick you up."

The land rippled and shook, knocking Chekov and his three companions flat. The shuttlecraft was still overhead. Chekov held his communicator close to his face. "Chekov to *Columbus*," he shouted, "do you think you can touch down just long enough to get us all aboard?"

"No," Sulu's voice replied, faintly.

"No!" Kirk said. "Sensors show more fissures are forming in that area. Looks like that thing's just waiting to grab the *Columbus*."

Chekov glanced at the green wall and suppressed a gasp of dismay. Another apparition was dislodging itself from the wall and coming forward.

This chimera was a giant cat, with thick black and white fur, but its face was that of Sergei Belyayev, his worst nightmare in primary school, a bully who liked to sidle up to him, slap his face, and laugh as he retreated. But why was that hated face on the body of a cat? How did a cat get into this mix of illusions?

"Banta!" Ojuremi cried out. Chekov did not understand what his cry meant, but guessed that the body of the cat might have been drawn from the Meropean man's memories.

"Stop it!" Aliss said. "You know it's not real, it can't be real!"

Real or not, the cat with the human face was unnerving as it snarled and showed Sergei's teeth. The illusion padded toward them, as if stalking its prey. Chekov looked up into the face of the childhood bully who had tormented him, and shivered. The face was grinning.

"Get away, you swine," Chekov shouted in Russian, unable to restrain himself, and in the next moment the shuttlecraft *Columbus* flew out from the cat's human head. But the face he had hoped never to see again continued to grin, then reached down with its paw, as if to bat him around and play with him. It isn't real, he reminded himself, and closed his eyes.

"How have you been all these years, Pavel?" Sergei asked, his voice deep inside Chekov's brain.

"What are you doing here?" Chekov asked, impressed in spite of himself by the strength of the illusion.

"I don't know, but it's fun, isn't it?" Sergei's voice said. "I wish I could touch you with my paw."

Chekov thought of a cat's sharp claws. "No!" he cried, understanding that the alien was searching his mind to find a way to strengthen the illusion, so that its violence might be felt as well as seen.

As Sulu circled the four human figures on the darkening plain, looking for a chance to land and rescue them, he saw the green wall become what seemed to be the hunched shoulders of an invading horde, all coming forward on foot. He had flown through the illusion of what looked like a giant cat, but now felt that the alien shaper was about to try for a more convincing simulacrum. Still, those strange black masses somehow gave him the feeling that the alien did not know quite how to form them, or was unsure whether or not they would frighten him.

Sulu brought the shuttlecraft around for another close pass. The giant cat was prowling around the four human figures below. The cat crouched and lashed out with one paw—

—and suddenly Sulu saw that the cat was tearing apart a screaming Chekov and biting into him with his teeth—

Sulu let out a curse as he passed low over the scene and then circled again for a better look. That cat isn't real, he told himself; therefore, it couldn't have eaten Pavel. He clung to that thought. The black masses still waited in the green wall. He swept around and caught sight of the cat, now consuming the remnants of Chekov. Uhura stood still, unmoving. Aliss was hanging on to Ojuremi, but the cat seemed uninterested in the two obviously horrified Meropeans or the apparently stunned Uhura. The fact that all three of them were seeing the same illusion he was indicated the strength of the mental cast.

"No!" Sulu said, determined to keep his self-control before the illusion's assault. "You can't fool me. It's all a lie."

The gigantic cat looked up at the shuttlecraft's approach, then reached up with its paw. Sulu had no time to turn away as the paw swatted at the *Columbus*. He felt the collision in his mind, heard the paw strike his craft, and shuddered as he passed through, hoping that there was nothing worse to come.

"Pavel," he muttered. Chekov had to be down there, alive. Then, as the view aft came up on his small viewscreen, he saw Chekov standing in full view, seemingly unharmed, motioning at him with one outstretched arm, and for a moment Sulu realized that he had doubted, that he had accepted what the illusion had shown him and had believed his shipmate lost.

Chapter Thirteen

"MR. SPOCK," Kirk said from his bridge command station, "what is to prevent a repeat of the attack on us, once our functions are restored?"

"I have anticipated that possibility," Spock said from his science station aft. "Mr. Scott and his team have finished placing barriers on all systems, and these barriers should be sufficient to block the kind of surge that was sent our way. The protection factor we have allowed for will protect us from a surge three times as powerful as the one we experienced. Still, we are assuming that the alien neural net will not be able to increase the strength of its surge without limit."

"And what about the crew?" Kirk asked. "Will the buffer protect us as well as our ship?"

"It should, up to that point. Again, I cannot predict the strength of a possible future attack."

Kirk stood up and gazed at the large viewscreen, where

the green biomass could still be seen around New Ibadan. Darkness would fall there soon. The people huddled in the square and on the terrace and waiting in the nearby buildings would be terrified as night cloaked their enemy. They would be fearing that dawn would show them the invader surging through their streets, spewing its cones of acid, as crevices opened up in the ground to swallow everything.

"If the mat attacks the city again," Kirk said, "we will have no choice but to open fire. Then, if our ship is attacked and disabled again, the city will be defenseless."

"True, Captain," Spock murmured, "and the biomass is moving again."

"Then there probably won't be time for other vessels to get here and help in any evacuation."

"No, Captain," Spock said. "There will definitely not be enough time for that."

Kirk sat down again. *"Enterprise* to *Columbus,"* he said.

"Columbus to *Enterprise,* Sulu here," the helmsman's voice answered. "I'm still circling the others. Unable to land and rescue. Every time I get within a couple of meters of the surface, cracks begin to form. Please advise."

"Keep circling for now," Kirk said, "and keep them all in sight."

"Aye, aye, sir."

"Jim," a familiar voice said from behind him.

Kirk glanced over his shoulder and saw McCoy leaving the lift, followed by Leander Cortés. "How are things in sickbay?" Kirk asked.

"We've got twenty crewmembers with broken limbs,"

the doctor replied, "four with concussions, and several others in shock but recovering. No fatalities, though. We were lucky."

"Yes, we were." Kirk glanced at Cortés. The captain of the *Hawking* had not been so fortunate with his comrades.

The viewscreen changed to show the view from the *Columbus.* Chekov, Uhura, Teressa Aliss, and Trent Ojuremi were tiny figures standing near the green wall, huddled close together, arms linked. As the ground rushed up toward Sulu's shuttlecraft, Kirk saw fissures beginning to form. Rifts opened and closed in seemingly random patterns.

"Good Lord," McCoy said as he gazed at the screen, "how is Sulu going to get them out of there?"

Kirk leaned forward. "Mr. Sulu," he said.

"Still here, Captain."

"Do you think you could land and make a pickup fast enough to avoid the cracks?"

"Unknown, Captain. I don't know how fast the alien mentality can make them open up."

Kirk glanced at McCoy.

"Don't look at me, Jim," McCoy said. "I wasn't much good at hopscotch as a boy." Kirk tried to smile, but knew that he had grimaced instead.

"The biomass has also been throwing illusions at us," Sulu continued, "giant cats and other chimeras. It could probably send another one at me to disorient me if I try to land."

"Captain Cortés," Kirk said, "did you see anything like those illusions?"

Cortés shook his head. "No, I didn't. As far as I know, nobody else who went out with me did, either."

"I can confirm that, sir," Longstreet said from the communications station. "The biomass threw acidic cones at us, but no illusions of any kind."

"Interesting," Spock said from his station. "The alien seems to be attempting another type of defense."

Kirk shook his head. Was the alien waiting for the shuttlecraft to land again, he wondered, readying to open the ground from under the *Columbus* as soon as Sulu touched down?

"Scotty?" Kirk said. "How are you progressing with the transporter?"

"Soon, Captain, soon," Scotty's voice answered.

"Mr. Sulu?" Kirk said. "Did you hear that?"

"Yes, Captain, but the question is how soon?"

"Lieutenant, you may have to make your own decision about what to do if this drags on. How much danger are the other four people in?"

"They're standing there and waiting," Sulu replied, "but fissures are forming only a few meters from them now. My feeling is that they could be swallowed at any moment."

Four lives against the shuttlecraft and Sulu, Kirk thought. Yet all five lives and the *Columbus* could be lost if he ordered Sulu to land.

"If the ground starts shaking," Sulu said, "and more rifts form, I may have no choice but to land. So maybe I should land and attempt a rescue right now while things seem relatively stable."

Kirk pressed his lips together and knew why he was in

command. A more prudent intellect would feel shackled and refuse the very condition of having to make dangerous choices. A more reckless intellect would completely ignore the risks.

Kirk considered the problem for a few moments, and finally asked himself exactly who was in a position to know the most about this dilemma, or to have feelings and intuitions that might be most useful in solving it.

Sulu, of course.

"Mr. Sulu," Kirk said, "use your own best judgment. That's an order."

Sulu decided that the risk was worth taking.

He brought the shuttlecraft down as close to the four human figures as possible—some seventy meters—and opened the entryway. His screen showed him four human figures making a desperate rush toward him.

The ground shook, rattling the shuttlecraft. Sulu saw Ojuremi slip into a narrow crack, but Chekov somehow managed to grab his arms and pull him back out. Aliss was hanging on to Uhura as they ran toward the shuttle-craft. He watched the four people disappear from his screen as they neared the shuttle entrance.

Sulu took a deep breath, waited, and then heard a loud thump behind him. He kept his eyes on his screen and control panel, not daring to turn his head even for an instant.

"We are all aboard!" Chekov shouted in back of him.

The ground suddenly heaved under the shuttlecraft, and Sulu felt the *Columbus* sinking, prow first. He would not be able to lift without causing damage, perhaps enough damage to disable his craft. The prow went down sixty degrees. Sulu looked back and saw Uhura and Chekov hanging on to the seats behind him to keep from falling on top of him while holding back Aliss and Ojuremi with their free arms.

The shuttlecraft slid down some more, and did not seem about to stop. If it keeps going, Sulu thought, we'll end up embedded in the ground.

"Enterprise!" Sulu shouted. "You'd better get us out right now! Five to beam up!"

There was no answer. The shuttlecraft's interior lights flickered, but he saw no obvious change in the vehicle—yet.

"Sulu to *Enterprise!"* he shouted again as the craft continued to slide. Its structure groaned as if in protest. "Beam us out of here!"

"Enterprise to *Columbus!"* Kirk's voice called out. "Ready for rescue. We're locked on to five, and can beam you up now."

"About time," Sulu muttered. As the cabin of the shuttlecraft faded from his view, he heard Chekov heave a sigh of relief.

"Five are aboard," someone was saying. Uhura recognized the voice of Lieutenant Kyle. "They're all safe, Captain Kirk."

As soon as she saw that she was on the transporter platform, Uhura looked around for Trent. His face was streaked with dirt and sagging with fatigue, but he was there, in the transporter chamber, standing next to Teressa Aliss.

A wave of relief rushed through her as she went to him. He took her hands, gripping them tightly.

They stepped down from the platform together. "We wouldn't have gotten out of there without you," Uhura said. "Our bodies would have been at the bottom of that fissure inside our vehicle."

Trent shook his head. "You were the one who told us we shouldn't wait, that we had to get out by ourselves."

Uhura glanced at Chekov and Sulu. "We have to go to the bridge," she said. "We may be needed there."

"We'll come with you, Lieutenant," Teressa said.

Uhura led them all out of the room and into the outside corridor. As they hurried toward the turbolift, she wondered what was happening on Merope IV. An alien force that could disable the *Enterprise,* swallow up settlements, threaten an entire planetary surface—there might be no way that they could hold it back, or save the colony.

"I shouldn't be here," Teressa said to Trent as they entered the turbolift. "I should be in New Ibadan with our people."

Uhura touched the other woman's shoulder. "The captain may need your counsel," she said.

"I hope we can stop the biomass," Chekov said, "but there were many moments down there when I was certain I would soon be reunited with Dmitri."

The lift doors opened. Uhura went onto the bridge, with the others behind her. Leander Cortés was on the bridge, standing next to the captain's command station.

Dr. McCoy came toward Uhura and her companions, scanned her quickly with his medical tricorder, then moved toward Sulu. "You're fit for duty, Uhura," the doctor murmured as he scanned the other lieutenant. "So are you, Sulu." He examined Chekov, waved the ensign away, then motioned to the First Citizen. "You and your aide should probably be in sickbay, Ms. Aliss." He scanned Teressa, then Trent. "Well, except for some pulled muscles, and rope burns on your hands, you don't seem in bad shape, either."

Uhura went to her communications station. Farley Longstreet got up, let her have her seat, and moved to Spock's science station to assist the Vulcan. A signal was coming in from Merope IV, Uhura noticed; Longstreet had already opened a channel to receive the call.

"Captain Kirk," Uhura said, "a call is coming in from New Ibadan." As she turned forward in her seat, the face of Dawn Voth appeared on the viewscreen.

"Teressa," the city councilwoman said, "you're safe."

Teressa went forward and stood near Captain Kirk and Leander Cortés. "Say what you have to say, Dawn," the First Citizen said.

"First Citizen and Captain Kirk," Dawn Voth said, "we have now evacuated everyone from the outer areas of the city and from the regions nearest the riverbank. The civic patrol and other volunteers are stationed along the perimeter with phasers set to disruption. This afternoon, it looked as though the growth had halted, but I've had reports from the patrol that it seems to be on the move again. Can you stop it?"

Captain Kirk stood up. "Ms. Voth," he said, "if the biomass keeps moving, we will attack it with the ship's phasers. I've also sent out a distress call for more vessels to come here and assist in evacuating your people."

Dawn Voth shook her head. "You couldn't possibly evacuate us all in time, not if that stuff—" She looked away for a moment.

"According to our sensor scans," Kirk said, "the people of your other settlements are safe at the moment." Uhura wondered if the captain was trying to offer Voth at least a little consolation with that statement of fact.

"For how long, Captain?" the councilwoman asked. "It's as if this thing deliberately aimed at our major population center first. How soon will this biomass be in our city streets? How soon will rifts start opening up and swallowing our buildings? And once we're gone, how long will the rest of our people remain safe?"

Mr. Spock turned toward the screen from his station. "According to my estimate," the Vulcan said, "at its present rate of movement, the green mat will reach the west, east, and north sides of the city in three hours and should be at the city center in ten hours."

Dawn Voth's mouth twisted. "In other words, by morning."

Teressa glanced toward Captain Kirk. Trent went forward to stand at the side of the First Citizen. "What are we going to do?" he asked.

Captain Kirk was silent.

Sulu took over his helmsman's station as Chekov sat down at the navigator's station. Sulu turned aft for a moment, aware of the tension on the bridge. "Sorry I lost that shuttlecraft, sir," he said to the captain.

Captain Kirk waved away the lieutenant's apology.

"We might retrieve it yet, and it's not as if Starfleet will send us a bill for it."

Sulu saw a quick smile on Cortés's face; even Ojuremi managed a muted laugh. For just a few moments, the tension had eased a bit.

"Captain," Teressa Aliss said then, "let me see what is happening below."

The screen view changed to show New Ibadan from above, surrounded by the green alien. Sulu noticed that the green stuff now covered much more of the southern riverfront.

"What are we going to do?" Aliss asked.

The captain rubbed his brow as he seated himself at his station. "If we fire on the mass again," he said, "and it disables our ship again, the city will be helpless and so will we."

"But do we have any choice except to fire?" Ojuremi said.

"That is what we must decide," Captain Kirk said. "We have barriers on our systems that should protect them, but we can't be certain that the safeguards we now have in place will shield us from the alien if it retaliates with greater force. Its first swat at us knocked out many of our functions, including the transporter."

"But you have taken precautions," the First Citizen said.

"To which the alien may respond by increasing the size of its attack pulse." Kirk turned toward her. "Every time it's attacked, it tries another defense—fissures in the ground, acid cones, illusions, destructive energy pulses—and it seems to have plenty of power to draw on."

"Yes," Aliss said, "that of our whole world."

"Then you propose to do nothing?" Ojuremi asked.

It seemed to Sulu then that the captain had no answer to the Meropean man's fearful question. For a moment, he wondered if he would finally see James Kirk face an unresolvable dilemma, a wall of damned-if-you-do and damned-if-you-don't bricks.

The image of the beleaguered city faded as the face of Dawn Voth reappeared. "Please help us," the council-woman said in a hoarse voice. "Do something—anything. We'll be fighting that stuff in our streets and inside our homes if you don't."

"If attacking it only makes the alien redouble its efforts," Kirk said, "then maybe an attack isn't the way to defeat it. Maybe it's time to try something else."

"That thing killed five of my shipmates . . . my friends," Cortés said. "How can you even suggest that we shouldn't keep fighting it?" But Sulu was already thinking that the captain's instincts might be telling him something. He had served on the *Enterprise* long enough to trust James Kirk's intuitions as much as he valued Spock's logic.

"Captain," Spock said then.

"What is it?" Kirk asked, glancing aft.

Spock was peering at his computer console. He turned from his station, got to his feet, and said, "I believe I have located the very heart of this alien neural net's vast planetary structure. It seems that the alien may have been attempting to shield that area from our sensors, but there is definitely a marked concentration of power there and our sensors are now picking it up."

The Vulcan came forward and stood near McCoy and Ojuremi. "These nodes lie only a few kilometers from the location of the settlement that was swallowed near the town of Shaku," Spock continued. "I request that I be allowed to beam into that position and attempt to contact the intelligence that rules the neural net."

"Is there any such intelligence?" McCoy asked, sounding skeptical.

"I am now convinced that there is," Spock said.

"And so am I," Teressa Aliss added. "After my recent experience, I am even more sure of that. The dreams that troubled so many Meropeans, the ones where we dreamed the same dream—maybe they were warnings. The alien might have been trying somehow to frighten us into leaving, and when we didn't, it attacked—first the settlement near Shaku, and now—" Her voice trailed off.

"Spock," Kirk said, "exactly what could you accomplish by beaming down there?"

"Destroy the thing," Cortés said. "That's what I'd do."

Spock lifted an eyebrow. "Of course that is not my intention," the Vulcan replied. "We have tried to do so, and have only provoked the alien into using more of its power against us."

"What did our colonists ever do to provoke such violence?" Ojuremi asked.

Spock said, "I suspect that it was the building of a settlement near the nodal crystallization of the neural net's general consciousness that elicited its violent response. It was on the basis of that hypothesis, together with knowing that the settlement was planning to increase in size—thus inevitably drawing more colonists into that area—that I was able to locate the sources of energy that I believe are at the heart of this planetary net."

"Then the proper course of action," Cortés said, "is to aim the *Enterprise*'s weapons at that spot and deliver the *coup de grâce*."

"I do not think so, Captain Cortés," Spock responded. "Instead, I mean to attempt a conversation."

Sulu sat back in his seat. "Is that even possible?" Dawn Voth asked from the screen, with wonder in her voice.

Spock shrugged. "Perhaps, perhaps not. My use of the word 'conversation' is optimistic."

"It's worth trying," Kirk said, assuming the constructive, probing manner that Sulu knew so well. The unknown would be made to yield its possibilities. If there was a way, it would be found.

"If you're willing to risk it, Commander Spock," Aliss said, "then I should go with you. This is my battle."

"That is precisely why I should go alone, Ms. Aliss," Spock said. "We do not wish to make the alien think that we are trying only to find another way to attack it. If I do not return, then Captain Kirk will have to decide whether or not to open fire on the green biomass surrounding New Ibadan in an attempt to save your city—or to buy the city enough time for other vessels to get here and evacuate your people."

Kirk sighed. "And you're sure that you don't want any company?" Sulu could tell from the sound of his voice that the captain very much wanted to be with his first officer.

"That is correct, Captain," the Vulcan said. "My concentration might be affected if I were to go as one of a team. There is also this possibility to consider. The alien might be willing to accept one individual as a peaceful envoy, while a group might be seen as a prelude to an enemy attack."

"And if we end up having to attack, my place is here, to give that order," Kirk said.

Spock nodded. "Exactly." He gestured toward his science station. "The location of the central node is well marked on my display."

"Will you go armed?" Kirk asked, but Sulu sensed that the captain already knew the answer to that question.

"No," Spock replied, "since that would only serve to provoke a being that already knows that I am a potential danger to it."

Teressa Aliss moved closer to Spock. "If I can't go with you, Commander," she said, "then I request that, before you leave, you beam me down to New Ibadan."

"I would strongly advise against that," Spock said. "Even having one person suddenly appear in a city under siege might be enough to make the alien feel more threatened, especially if another individual then materializes near its neural center."

"Mr. Spock is right," Kirk said as he gazed at the First Citizen. "And if his plan doesn't work, I doubt that any of us would be much safer here than we would be down there."

"Commander Spock, if this works, we'll all be grateful to you," Dawn Voth said. "I'll tell the other council members what you're doing. Voth out." Her face vanished, to be replaced by a view of the Meropean city at dusk. Sulu narrowed his eyes; he could not be certain, but it looked as though the green mat had moved even closer to New Ibadan's eastern and western sides.

Sulu turned around in time to see Spock heading toward the turbolift. The lift opened, Spock stepped inside, and the door slid shut behind him.

Everyone on the bridge was silent for a few moments. "What will you do when he fails?" Ojuremi asked, sounding both angry and fearful.

Captain Kirk stood up. "If he fails, I will open fire on the alien and we will all take our chances with the consequences. Surely you know that, Mr. Ojuremi, but if you have another idea, I would like to hear it."

Ojuremi looked away for a moment. "I am sorry, Captain. I know that you are doing everything you can. It's just that Teressa and I would rather be down there, with our people, instead of waiting here."

"As would I," Cortés said, "and my comrades would tell you the same thing." He gazed at Captain Kirk. "And if Merope Four needs us as fighters later on, I hope you'll beam me back down to the city to help clear that mat."

Teressa Aliss put a hand on Cortés's arm. "You've proven your loyalty to our world," she said. "I know very well that for every one of your comrades who went out with you, several more wanted the chance."

Sulu saw the mixed emotions in the troubled eyes of the man from the past. Part of Cortés wanted Spock to succeed, but the rest of the man would be itching to go back and destroy the thing that had taken the lives of five of his comrades. Then Sulu glanced at the captain, and knew that Kirk's heart and mind were with Spock in the transporter room, with his friend as he beamed down into the planetary alien. Kirk was staring at the turbolift as if wanting to follow; then he turned forward once more.

"Lieutenant Longstreet, take over Mr. Spock's station," Kirk said in a clear, strong voice. "I want an exact pinpoint of the coordinates where Spock is beamed down. I want that place scanned continuously. I want him watched by all of you for the slightest hint that we have to get him out of there. Understood?"

No one needed to answer.

Chapter Fourteen

THE WORLD THAT SOLIDIFIED before Spock's eyes was a twisting forest of greens, blues, and reds. Thick red and blue arteries snaked around a massive trunk that went up for at least a hundred meters. The air was humid and dank, almost unbreathable according to his tricorder readings, but there was enough oxygen to sustain him.

He stood perfectly still, placed his hands on one thick artery, and reached out with his mind to the sentience in the great trunk . . .

. . . and felt its puzzlement. It had come to be in the complexities of its structure, and was a mystery to itself; but it had protected itself, growing and becoming and seeking to know.

That, Spock told himself, declared this being as kin to all other intelligence in the universe.

He sensed a kind of surprise and wonder in the alien—that there were other beings who thought but were not at all like itself. They did not possess a world, as it did in its growing grasp. They came from outside and were not bound, as it was, to the soil and crust of the planet. They moved across the surface, and above it.

But now, one had appeared without crawling or treading or alighting from above. Suddenly another being was here, and this entity had not revealed how it had arrived. The alien was looking for a way to explain Spock to itself.

Spock, concentrating his thoughts, made it known that the intelligence was welcome to reach out to him without danger. He did so through alternating images, projected in the hope that one would convince. The first image was of a humanoid holding a round object in his hands; the second was of himself, stretching out his arms and extending empty hands, palms up.

I have come to you with no intent to harm you, Spock insisted in his mind. I have brought no weapons, and nothing else with which to strike out at you. I have come only to share my thoughts with you.

Then, as his eyes adjusted to the deep-blue-green glow, he peered around, trying to see farther into the alien structure. He was in an underground forest, under what looked like a low sky, trying to see between closely set trees, except that here, there were no paths among them.

Suddenly, a shadowy figure moved among the trunks and snaking vines. The shape seemed familiar—so much so that, for a moment, Spock suspected that he was seeing his own reflection in the heavy haze. But he knew that this could not be the case, since he was standing still and the figure was moving.

Slowly, the shape moved toward him, and he saw that it was tall and humanoid, but still a silhouette in the gloom. Spock took a deep breath in surprise as he saw that the figure was himself. The other Spock came to a halt and gazed at him with the characteristically curious and critical examination that Spock knew so well in himself.

"We have had great difficulty," his simulacrum said, "in finding a way to talk to you. You are very alien."

Spock nodded. "We are alien to each other. Were my emanations helpful?"

"Yes," said his other. "They allowed us to present ourselves to you in this form. But we are still uncertain."

Spock noticed then that the alien, although in a uniform like his own, had no ship's insignia on his blue shirt. As that thought came to him, a v-shaped symbol resembling the insignia slowly appeared on his simulacrum's uniform.

"I am here to communicate with you, both on my own behalf and for others," Spock said. "I am curious about you, but also wish to make assurances that the constructions and excavations of the surface dwellers were not meant to harm you."

He heard the whisper of a sigh, and then a low, throbbing sound. The sound was apparently coming from the treelike structures near him. Spock listened, trying to place the sound, which reminded him of a heartbeat.

"Constructions?" his simulacrum asked. "Excavations?" The other Spock lifted a brow. "Your meaning is becoming clearer to us. You are telling us of the scars the surface dwellers make in the ground and the things that they raise upon the land, things that do not live and breathe, that do not dig down into the soil with roots, but simply stand there on the surface."

Spock said, "The surface dwellers did not intend to harm you."

"That is what we thought . . . believed . . . concluded," Spock's likeness murmured. "The surface dwellers made their marks upon the land and put up their objects, yet they also tended and nurtured much of the other life that grew upon the surface or that lived all around them. We found this. . . ." The simulacrum paused and stared at Spock with questioning eyes.

"You found it puzzling?" Spock asked. "Confusing?"

"Incomprehensible. We considered how to reach out to them. We sent out . . . emanations . . . to see if we could touch them, communicate with them. We found that many could receive our emanations during the dark times, when they cease to move and stay inside the objects they have put up on the surface. But we felt resistance in them, and fear. They recoiled from us when we reached out to them. They did not want to become part of us. They did not understand us."

That, Spock thought to himself, might explain the dreams and nightmares that had troubled so many of the colonists.

"Yes," his simulacrum said, "we sent out what you call dreams, but when the surface dwellers did not accept them, we withdrew, to contemplate and consider what to do, how else to reach out. That is what we would still be doing if they had not threatened us directly."

"They did not mean to harm you," Spock said. "Why do you say that you were threatened?"

"They were getting so close to us . . . to me," the other Spock replied.

"To you?"

"To our . . . to my . . . most central place. The oldest, where all that cannot come again might be lost if it were destroyed . . . the place where all that was carved out and made limited of the infinite . . . exists."

The settlement near Shaku, Spock thought; the neural net, then, had attacked it because the community was too close to its nodes. The alien, as he had hypothesized earlier, had believed that it was acting in its own self-defense.

Spock looked into his own face and found it inscrutable, concealing an alien presence. How might he understand this other being, beyond its words, so that he would be certain of whatever accord might be reached? Was there within his human half a brief flicker of that intuitive sense, that ability to move into the unknown on the basis of inadequate evidence that had served James Kirk so well?

In Captain Kirk's determined expression, Teressa saw a man in full control of himself and his ship. From time to time he would ask one of the officers on the bridge a question, but for the past hour the captain had mostly been still and silent, waiting. She had no doubt that he would act decisively if it proved necessary, that he would do whatever was possible to save New Ibadan and her world.

The *Enterprise* would probably fire upon the green mat surrounding the city first, to give the alien one last chance to withdraw. After that, Captain Kirk would have to use phaser fire against the location where his first officer had beamed down to confront the nodes of the neural net. If the transporter officers failed to beam him out of danger in time, Commander Spock would certainly die in such an attack, and Teressa sensed that James Kirk would mourn Spock's loss very deeply.

Dr. McCoy was still standing at Kirk's right. "Jim," he said, "I'm not of much use here. I might as well head back to sickbay and see how my patients are doing. I'm sure Spock can take care of himself—he's rugged enough." In spite of the doctor's casual manner, Teressa saw that he was also worrying about his fellow officer. McCoy glanced aft. "What's going on with him down there?"

"No change," Lieutenant Longstreet said from the science station. "Mr. Spock is still in the location where he beamed down."

"That has to be a good sign," Teressa said. The captain glanced at her from his station. "It means that the alien didn't strike out at him, that it might be listening to what he has to say."

"Or that it's simply considering how best to get rid of him," Leander Cortés said, "or perhaps that it's immobilized him somehow."

McCoy went to the turbolift; the door closed behind him. Trent stood near Uhura's station, gazing at the forward viewscreen. Captain Kirk's eyes were on the screen, where another aerial view of New Ibadan could be seen.

"Our sensor readings," the captain said, "indicate that the growth has slowed in its advance around the city. Perhaps the alien is holding back and waiting to hear what Mr. Spock has to say."

"I doubt it," Cortés muttered.

"Captain Cortés," Kirk said, "if you have any other recommendations to offer, please do."

"Beam Commander Spock out of there and burn that location out with phaser fire."

"Not until there is no other alternative," Kirk replied.

Teressa stepped closer to Cortés. "We haven't given Spock enough time yet," she said to him. "As long as nothing seems to have changed, we can wait a little longer."

"We might end up waiting too long," Cortés said. "That thing killed five of my friends. Nothing you do now is going to bring them back."

"It killed over one hundred of my people," Teressa said. "A few were people I knew, and all of them were people for whom I was responsible. Nothing can bring them back, either."

Cortés regarded her in silence for a few moments. "I suppose you must think of me as a remnant of Earth's violent past."

"I think of you as a man who has lost friends and who is grieving for them," she said. "I don't object to your feelings, Leander—they're understandable. But we can't let anger and a desire for revenge determine our actions now."

"Captain," Longstreet said then, "there's something odd about the area around Mr. Spock. The sensors are indicating the possible presence of other life-forms besides the alien and the commander."

Captain Kirk looked aft. "Are you sure?"

"That's just it. I can't be sure. There seems to be some sort of field intermittently blocking the sensors. We've kept a constant scan on Mr. Spock since he beamed down, but—"

Ensign Chekov turned around at his station. "The alien was able to send a powerful pulse of energy against the *Enterprise*. It managed to show me a monstrous cat wearing the face of a boy who used to torment me. Maybe it can fool our vessel's sensors as well."

"Mr. Chekov," Kirk said, "that's quite a leap, given that our sensors didn't pick up any readings from the illusions that afflicted you and Sulu. For now, we had better assume those sensor readings are real, and that they might be an indication of other life-forms with some connection to the alien nodes."

But if that was the case, Teressa wondered, then why had those life-forms appeared there now, so close to Mr. Spock?

The alien simulacrum was leading him through what appeared to be masses of twisting vines. Spock followed, still hearing the low-pitched sound of a giant beating heart.

The simulacrum halted in a space filled with a thick green fog. "You are different," the alien said, "from the beings on the surface, and yet you are also like them."

"Yes, that is so." Spock waited, to see if more explanation would be required from him, but the alien was silent.

Through the fog, he glimpsed more trees of the alien forest. But that was not the way to think of this place, he thought to himself. The trees, the vines—all of them were a part of this alien organism; all of them were fed by the nodes of the neural net.

He turned toward the other Spock. "The people of the surface," Spock continued as he peered into his own face, "have no wish to harm you, no motive to do so, nothing to gain. We can mark this central place, so that it will never be approached. We can find ways to ensure that you and the surface dwellers can live peacefully together."

The face of the simulacrum betrayed no answer to his words, but Spock sensed that the alien was struggling with the possibility of deception. That was a new idea to this being; nothing had ever attempted to deceive it in the past. But then how had it arrived at the notion to send illusions out against Sulu and Chekov, in order to delude and frighten them?

"Others came down and alighted on the surface," the other Spock said. "We searched inside them for images through which we might touch them somehow, and yet . . ." The simulacrum gave an oddly familiar shrug of the shoulders.

The illusions, then, had been other attempts by the alien to communicate, but they had gone wrong. Spock reminded himself that the alien had responded only when fired upon, after its vital territory had been invaded.

"We have a request to make of you," Spock said. "In return for promising to protect your central place, we ask that you withdraw from around the large aggregation of beings and structures that is the central place of the surface dwellers, the city that they call New Ibadan."

His other said, "But do you not have the power to destroy us from the sky?"

Spock nodded. "Possibly, but you can then respond as you did before, and it is not clear that we would be able to stop you. Even if we could, more surface dwellers would die. Enough have died already."

Confusion passed across the visage of the other Spock. "Died?"

"Ceased to exist," Spock said. "You have killed some of the surface dwellers, and yet all of us are willing to put that aside if we can live with you in peace from now on."

"Killed? Dead?" The other Spock drew his brows together. "But they are not dead. We . . . cradle them."

Spock grasped at this unexpected chance. "If that is so," he said, "and if they can be returned to the surface, the matter will be resolved."

His simulacrum turned away from him. Spock waited, listening to the whirl of incomprehensible alien thoughts whispering through him.

Dawn Voth's image was on the bridge screen. Kirk saw the shadows under her eyes, and the lines around her mouth seemed more deeply etched.

"I've had more reports," the councilwoman said. "The volunteers waiting to defend the perimeter say that the biomass hasn't moved for at least an hour."

"Our sensor readings confirm that," Kirk said.

"Then do you think your Mr. Spock has actually been able to—persuade it to hold off?"

"We can assume that for now, Ms. Voth," Kirk replied. "But he's been there for half the night already."

"All indications are that he's safe," Kirk said, "so at the moment, there's no need to fire upon the invader. The fact that the biomass hasn't advanced is a hopeful sign."

Dawn Voth sighed. "Captain, let me be blunt. We've got everyone in the city crowded into the center, terrified. Sooner or later, at least a few of our volunteers will take matters into their own hands and start attacking and trying to clean out that biomass."

Teressa Aliss stepped forward. "They mustn't," she said, "not while there's still a chance to settle this peaceably."

"Ms. Voth," Kirk said, "be assured that if the biomass begins to move again, we will fire upon it. I don't want any members of your patrols any closer to the perimeter than they already are, or they may be in danger from our phaser fire."

He sat back, worrying about whether or not Spock was making any progress with the alien . . . and when the green growth might again resume its attack on New Ibadan.

Spock waited as his simulacrum vanished into a mass of blue and green vines. The throbbing sound was softer now, but the fog was beginning to clear, revealing what seemed to be a mossy green path that led toward another wall of vines.

The vines suddenly parted and his counterpart reappeared. The other Spock was not alone this time; a man stood with him, a stocky dark-eyed man with short thick hair and sharp cheekbones, a man Spock knew.

"Dmitri Sergeievich Glakov," Spock said as he moved toward the man, "I am most astonished to see you alive."

Glakov's brown eyes widened. "No more surprised than am I, Commander Spock. I thought that I was finished when the ground swallowed me and my vehicle, and then—" He turned and looked at the other Spock. "Am I speaking to the right person?"

"This one appeared here suddenly, within us," the simulacrum said. "It is the one from outside. I am merely a means of communicating with this creature."

Spock realized that this Glakov might be an illusion, an apparition like the chimeras that had been thrown at Chekov and Sulu, but the man seemed too real for that, and then Glakov came toward him and clasped his hands. "I am real," Glakov said, gripping him firmly. "Let me assure you of that."

"I must assure myself of that," Spock said as Glakov released him. He turned toward his alien self. "I have brought an instrument with me, a tricorder. It is not a weapon. May I use it now to verify that this man is truly present?"

The simulacrum was silent for several moments. "You may direct your instrument at this being."

Spock scanned Glakov quickly. "Yes," he said as he read the tricorder readings, "you are indeed the man I see before me. What happened to you?"

"I was in my vehicle, trapped in darkness so black that I could not see," the Russian said. "I could hear the mass eating through the hood with its acids. Rachel was up by the controls, she might have been screaming. I can't be certain of that, because I was screaming so much myself that I wouldn't have heard her voice over my own cries, and then I felt this . . . this warm viscous *stuff* flowing onto me."

Glakov paused. The other Spock watched him impassively, showing no reaction.

"I believed that it would dissolve me, disintegrate me," Glakov continued. "By then, I was so numb, so tired from screaming out my terror, that I could feel nothing. I kept expecting to feel a burning as the acid ate into me, but after a few moments, I realized that I was still alive, even though I was soon entirely encased in this warm, moist cocoon. Of course that was even more terrifying to me."

"Indeed," Spock murmured. Glakov had no doubt been thinking of Earth's spiders and of how they wrapped and immobilized their prey before devouring them.

"But as I lay there," Glakov continued, "a feeling of calm, of restfulness and peace, came over me. I felt—not happy exactly, but tranquil and serene. This was not at all reassuring at first—I can tell you that. I had the notion that the biomass, or whatever was controlling it, might only be sedating me until it was ready to devour me. Then dreams began to come to me."

"Dreams?" Spock asked.

"Of losing myself, of forgetting, of having memories drift away from me, of being very slowly absorbed by something else . . . and yet I wasn't afraid. Whatever had encased me did not mean me any harm—that came through quite clearly."

"It sounds," Spock said, "as though the alien was trying to communicate with you."

"Yes," the other Spock murmured, "that is true. We felt a strong resistance in this being to becoming part of us, in this being and in the others we have kept cradled. We have felt some of their emanations, have learned a little more about those who move over the ground and upon it. But what shall we do with them now? What will happen to the ones we cradle and to us if the surface dwellers attack us again?"

"They will not attack you," Spock said, "if you withdraw from the city—the aggregation of the surface dwellers that you have surrounded. They will promise not to encroach on your central place as long as you leave them in peace. As for those you are cradling, may I suggest that they might make excellent intermediaries."

"Intermediaries?" the other Spock said, lifting a brow.

"Yes," Spock replied, "another way for you to communicate with the surface dwellers and achieve peace with them, a link to those who are unlike yourself. But first you will have to let them go."

It would be dawn in New Ibadan soon, Kirk thought, and there was still no word from Spock. The bridge viewscreen showed a city surrounded by the alien growth, although the biomass was still not advancing.

"Commander Spock is now seventy meters away from the point where he first beamed down," Longstreet reported from the science station, "and I am picking up more life-form readings near him."

A decision would have to be made soon. Kirk longed

to try to contact Spock, to ask him what was going on, but knew that such an action might only alarm the alien and provoke it into a defensive response.

"Captain Kirk," Trent Ojuremi called out; he was standing near Uhura's station. "How much longer are we going to wait?"

Kirk glanced back at the man. Everyone on the bridge looked tired, but Ojuremi and the First Citizen were clearly fighting exhaustion. Teressa Aliss now sat on the floor near Leander Cortés, her shoulders slumped forward, while Ojuremi's reddened eyes betrayed a man badly in need of sleep.

"We will wait as long as necessary," Kirk said. "I remind you that the longer things remain as they are, the more time there is for other Starfleet vessels to get here to help your people. In the meantime, I suggest that you and Ms. Aliss get some food and some sleep. I can summon a couple of yeomen to show you to temporary quarters."

Teressa Aliss lifted her head. "No, thank you," she said softly. "I'll stay here." Kirk admired her for her determination to keep watch over her world, even though she had to know that she could accomplish nothing by remaining on the bridge.

"You can't fool me," Ojuremi said. "Even if other ships get here in time, they can't possibly evacuate everyone."

Uhura reached out and tugged at Ojuremi's sleeve. He looked down at her for a moment. "Excuse me, Captain," Ojuremi said, "I guess I'm tired."

Uhura turned back to her console, then said, "Captain,

a call is coming in from—" Before the lieutenant could finish, Kirk heard the voice of his first officer.

"Spock to *Enterprise*."

"Spock!" Kirk gripped the arms of his chair. "What's going on?"

"I have established communication with the alien, Captain, and was successful in my negotiations. Ready to beam up."

"Captain!" Chekov shouted from his station. "Our sensor readings show that the biomass is retreating from New Ibadan!"

Teressa Aliss was suddenly on her feet. On the screen, Kirk clearly saw the green growth slowly withdrawing from around the city.

"It's leaving," the Meropean woman murmured. "I can hardly believe it."

"Captain Kirk." That was Scotty's voice. "Mr. Spock is safely aboard, and on his way to the bridge."

As relieved as Kirk was to see Spock come onto the bridge, he was also extremely curious about what his friend had discovered, and exactly what kind of agreement he had managed to secure from the alien.

"Mr. Spock," Teressa Aliss said as she went to Spock, "you have saved our world," and took one of the Vulcan's hands in both of hers.

Spock looked down at Aliss, as if unsure of how to react, then released his hand from her clasp. "It is fortunate that the alien was acting in self-defense," he said, "and that it was therefore willing to communicate with me. What triggered its aggression was the encroachment of your people on its central space, its nodal area, when a new settlement was built near Shaku. As long as you agree to keep away from that region, where the alien feels most vulnerable, your communities will be safe."

"And that's all we have to do?" Ojuremi asked.

Spock lifted a brow. "We must not expect a more discursive agreement with the planetary alien."

"Sounds straightforward enough to me," Kirk said, although he was curious about the details.

"Not to me," Ojuremi responded, looking doubtful. "Commander Spock, you are being evasive."

Spock shrugged. "Not at all. I am simply reporting what happened at the level of precision that is possible."

"But will we be safe?" Teressa Aliss asked.

"Yes," Spock said. "New Ibadan is no longer threatened, as you can see on the screen."

Leander Cortés stepped up to Spock, his dark eyes fierce with anger. "So now we have to live with this thing that killed five of my comrades," he said, "and forget what happened. I don't know if I have the stomach to live on such a world."

Spock lifted a brow. "No one has died, Captain Cortés."

"What?" Ojuremi said. Cortés's eyes widened.

"Those who were lost are not dead," Spock continued. "The alien explained to me that it has, so to speak, cradled them and kept them safe inside itself. I spoke to your comrade Dmitri Sergeievich Glakov, and—"

"Dmitri?" Chekov cried out, then quickly rose to his feet. "He's alive?"

"Indeed he is," Spock replied. "The alien is willing to

release all of those it is cradling in return for a promise to leave its central area untouched and protected." Kirk saw Spock's eyes narrow slightly as he gazed at Cortés. "Had we aimed our phasers at the alien's nodal region, and succeeded in destroying it, the lives of those people would have been lost as well."

Cortés shook his head, looking confused.

"How wonderful that they're safe," Teressa Aliss murmured. She turned toward Cortés. "Maybe you'll want to stay on our world now."

"You lost more people than I did," Cortés said, "and yet you're still—"

"Obviously my meaning was not clear to you," Spock interrupted. "The alien has not only been cradling Captain Cortés's companions, but also all of those who were believed killed when the settlement near Shaku was destroyed. No lives at all were lost."

The mingled joy and bewilderment on the First Citizen's face showed Kirk that she was having trouble believing this revelation. For that matter, he still had some doubts of his own.

"Spock," Kirk said, "can you be sure of this? The alien was capable of creating illusions that seemed very real to those who saw them."

Ojuremi nodded. "Exactly what I wanted to ask."

"But we also do have sensor readings," Kirk went on, "indicating that other life-forms were present where Spock beamed down."

"Yes," Spock said, "and I am certain that the Glakov to whom I spoke is no illusion. The alien allowed me to scan him with my tricorder, so that I could confirm that fact.

In any case, Ms. Aliss will soon have the opportunity to verify what the alien told me. It intends to release those it holds outside Shaku. I have promised that we will be there to welcome them."

"We?" Kirk asked.

"I am willing to be present, and the First Citizen should accompany me, as the representative of her people, along with Captain Cortés, since he—"

"Wait," Ojuremi said. "Teressa, how do we know this isn't a trick, another way the alien may be trying to defend itself? Perhaps it means to lure you there with false promises so that it can strike against us again."

"Trent," Aliss said, "everything the alien has done since Commander Spock beamed down indicates that it's sincere about seeking a peace with us. If it is trying to deceive us, I had better find that out now, and if our lost people are returned to us, that will only confirm the alien's good faith. We must have facts from which to reason and make our decisions." She gazed at her aide in silence for a few moments, then looked away. "I am willing to beam down with you, Mr. Spock. Before we leave, we should also let the council members in Shaku know what's going on, since it was their people who unknowingly built that settlement over the alien's central place."

Ojuremi sighed. "Teressa, if you're going to go, I should come with you."

"So will I," Cortés added.

"And so will I," Kirk said as he got to his feet. "Mr. Sulu, take command."

Sulu stood up. "I have one question before you go. Mr. Ojuremi, do you happen to have a cat?"

Trent Ojuremi frowned. "As a matter of fact, I do—or did, assuming she's still somewhere safe in the city."

Sulu smiled. "That's all I wanted to know."

Messanga Watson, the councilman of Shaku, was waiting for Kirk and his companions when they beamed down. A large brown-skinned man, he was quick to greet them, obviously eager to have peace in his world once more.

"Teressa, I am relieved to see you." Watson stepped away from his land vehicle and pressed his hand against the First Citizen's palm in greeting. "I had to come out here after I got your message." He glanced at Kirk. "My daughter was one of those who was in the settlement we lost. If she truly is alive—"

"I am certain that she is," Spock said.

They were standing on a small hill overlooking a grassy plain. In the distance, less than a kilometer away, was a forested hill of trees that resembled Earth's pines and larches. Beyond that, to the north, lay the alien's central place. Kirk glanced at Teressa Aliss and Leander Cortés; the same expressions of hope and apprehension played across both their faces.

Trent Ojuremi cupped a hand over his eyes. "I see something out there."

"So do I," Kirk said. A few people were coming out from the distant trees. Others followed them, among them children and three women carrying babies. Kirk soon recognized the stocky form of Dmitri Glakov and Rachel Zlatopolsky's long black braid.

"Emo," Cortés said, "I see Emo. He's alive, he didn't die."

Spock took out his tricorder. "Scanning now," he said. "My readings indicate that those we see are indeed human life-forms."

"Miriam!" Messanga Watson cried out. "My daughter! She's with them!" The councilman was suddenly running toward the returning people, waving his arms as he bounded through the high grass.

"They're alive," Teressa Aliss said softly.

Cortés turned toward Kirk and Spock. "I was wondering, Mr. Spock," the captain of the *Hawking* murmured, "if you have any more thoughts about this . . . this strange reality we have to live with."

"Yes," Aliss added. "Why do you think it has chosen to—well, to tolerate us and live with us?"

"I would not characterize it in quite that way," Spock said. "I would say that it is interested in the company."

"Company?" Ojuremi asked.

Spock was silent for a moment, then said, "It might be closer to the truth to say that the alien has been alone for as long as it can remember. As with all sentient life, it is unable to solve the riddle of existence. Now it has its own other—alien intelligences of whom it might ask the question: What do you think of it all?"

"In other words," Kirk said, "it wants to find out how we're doing on all the great questions."

Spock nodded. "As it has formulated those questions for itself. As long as the settlers on Merope Four agree to share the planet—and after all, the alien was here first— then there will be nothing to fear. In time, we may learn something from such a sentience. Dmitri Glakov tells me that, while the alien was cradling him, he had a strong

208

impression that he was being held by the mind of a world, an intelligence so ancient that it may be as old as the planet itself."

Kirk saw a smile form on Teressa Aliss's face. "So we will have an actual Gaia," she said, "a planetary mother."

"You might put it that way," Spock said.

Teressa reached for Kirk's hand. Out in the field, Messanga Watson was embracing a young woman and the baby she held in her arms.

Chapter Fifteen

"IT'S GOING TO BE hard for me to leave here," Uhura said to Trent.

"It will be hard to see you go," he replied.

They sat on a bench in a garden overlooking the west end of Yakuru Plaza, near the location where, she knew, Trent hoped a university complex would rise one day. So far, he and his small faculty were holding classes in two buildings barely larger than houses; but the school would grow, and already had nearly one hundred students, with even more hoping to join them in the future.

Banta, Trent's cat, leaped out from a bed of bright red flowers that looked like peonies, rubbed against Uhura's leg, then curled up at her feet. The animal, apparently unaffected by the city's recent siege, had been waiting for Trent outside the building that housed the city council offices and living quarters when he had returned to the city.

Uhura reached down and scratched the cat behind

the ears; Banta purred. "I'm sure we'll be back here eventually," she said. "Captain Kirk will want to see how the new colonists from the *Hawking* are getting along later on."

"I think they'll do very well," Trent said. "They've already won our respect. Leander Cortés and a few others promised to speak to some of our history students."

Across the plaza, Captain Kirk was out for a stroll with Teressa Aliss. He and the First Citizen would have a few last bits of business to settle, and Uhura also knew that the captain had welcomed an excuse to spend more time with such a beautiful woman. Uhura breathed in the clear, slightly cool air of Merope IV and felt content. This colony would thrive, and she could leave knowing that Trent had made a good life for himself here.

She had not been entirely honest with Trent or, she supposed, with herself. She had told him that she had no regrets about her past decisions; but there had in fact been one lingering regret for years: that she had remained unreconciled with Trent. Now, that last wound had finally been healed.

Chekov walked along the riverbank with Glakov. Except for barren patches of ground where gardens had once thrived and brown masses of residue where buildings had stood, there were few signs of the biomass that had infested the river and the city. The green invader had retreated, leaving behind itself the clear blue water of the swiftly flowing river and empty spaces where new structures would soon be raised.

"You will be even more of a legend now, Uncle Mitya,"

Chekov said, "when I go home to tell the rest of the family about what happened to you and about your adventures here."

Dmitri Glakov smiled. "It is good to know that I have a chance to be remembered as more than a colorful Moscow criminal."

"That reputation had its uses, Uncle Mitya. My mother and father often told me that I had better work hard so that I would not become such a rogue."

Glakov's expression grew more solemn. "Never in all of the years that I was aboard the *Hawking* and crossing black space did I ever imagine what lay ahead for me. I have been dreaming during the past nights."

"Dreaming?" Chekov asked.

"I have dreams of being absorbed, of being drawn into something much more vast, inside a being that encompasses a world. I feel that I am losing parts of myself, and yet I am not afraid, and I always find myself again when I awake." He stopped walking and turned to face Chekov. "I spoke to Rachel about my dreams, and hers are the same as mine. She says that all of us who were captured—who were cradled—seem to be having the same dreams. We think that they may be a part of what the alien, the mind of this world, is trying to teach us."

Glakov was silent for a while. Chekov stood with him, looking out over the river at the opposite bank, where a profusion of colorful flowers now bloomed on the plain over which the green mat had moved.

"It will be interesting," Chekov said at last, "to see what this world is like many years from now."

"That it will," Glakov said. "I am pleased that I will be

a small part of it. I only wish that I could live long enough to learn all that the alien might teach us."

"These were my quarters," Rachel Zlatopolsky said to Scotty as she led him into a small cubicle. "I shared them with Laure Vidor, and I can't say I'll be unhappy to see the last of them."

Looking around the tiny room, with its two narrow shelf-like beds that could be pushed into the walls and its small retractable desk and ancient screen, Scotty could well understand her sentiments. Even one person would have felt cramped in such quarters, and Rachel had lived in them with the other woman for many long years. Toward the end, he thought, she must have believed herself to be lying down in a place that would become her coffin every time she came here to sleep.

Yet he felt an affection for the old hulk, for the vessel that had carried Leander Cortés and his shipmates so far from Earth. She's a good old craft, Scotty told himself, thinking of the engines that had worked so hard during the *Hawking*'s journey and which had finally failed through no fault of their own.

Scotty made a quick scan of the room with his tricorder and the other equipment he had brought aboard, then stepped out into the corridor. Rachel followed him from the room, pulling the metal door shut behind her.

"Are you sure about what you decided?" Scotty asked, even though he had asked her that same question earlier.

"Yes, we are," Rachel said. "It's necessary—we all agreed on that. Leander put the proposal before all of us, and there wasn't a single dissenting vote."

"Aye," Scotty said, "you're probably right, lassie, but rest assured that this old ship won't be forgotten."

As the crew of the *Enterprise* made final preparations to leave the Meropean system, Kirk sat at his command station considering what he might have overlooked. He had made his report to Starfleet; the starships on their way to join him had been ordered to turn back. Several of the people from the *Hawking* were already building new homes for themselves on the outskirts of the city or along the riverbank. Teressa Aliss and the New Ibadan city council had entertained him and his officers with as fine a banquet as he had ever enjoyed.

McCoy was on the bridge, standing at Kirk's right, staring at the viewscreen. As Spock came and stood at the captain's left, Kirk looked up and asked, "Are we all ready?"

"All is in order, Captain," Spock said.

"Mr. Spock," Kirk said, "now that it's over, what do you think of this encounter?"

Spock clasped his hands behind him and gazed at the image of Merope IV on the bridge screen. "There were, of course, two problems to solve," the Vulcan said, "the settling of the people from the *Hawking* on a new world, and the emergent problem of the planetary intelligence, whose detection might have been delayed by some years if we had not brought the *Hawking*'s people here."

Kirk smiled. "And I must say that I find it refreshing that these people out of time, who were seeking a new world, have now chosen not to cling to their past, but to renounce its unfortunate aspects in their new home."

Spock nodded. "Yes, Captain. Refreshing, and unexpected."

"What you mean to say," Kirk said, "is . . . especially in a species that has so often glorified violence in its history."

Spock turned toward him for a moment. "Yes, Captain. Thank you for finishing my thought."

"It will be hard for them," McCoy said. "I can't help feeling that a few of them will never come out of that lonely deep where they spent so much of their lives."

Kirk glanced at the physician. "Do you think it will be really bad for them?"

McCoy sighed. "People are adaptable, and maybe what some of them learn from the planetary alien will help to banish some of their darker thoughts."

"Yes," Kirk said, "and they showed their courage, even if some of them will carry the darkness within themselves for the rest of their lives. There will be enough daylight for them here."

But even as he spoke, Kirk imagined Cortés, for whom he had developed such a liking and respect, waking in the night, still trapped aboard a drifting ship, with no help anywhere. The old starship had been launched like a javelin across the universe, only to slow forever in the blackness without finding its mark. . . .

It might have been so.

But it was not.

Kirk glanced first at Spock, then McCoy, and said, "Scotty, are we ready?"

"Aye, Captain," Scotty's voice replied, "the *Hawking* is now far enough away for the job to be done."

The image of Merope IV vanished; the main screen now showed the distant *Hawking* in its sunward orbit. Scotty had made a complete three-dimensional scan of the ship for the record; in several weeks, the starship would approach the sun and be vaporized, but that had not been enough for Leander Cortés. A greater gesture was needed to help along the life of his people in their new world.

Suddenly, silently, the *Hawking* exploded. Its brightness lingered for a few moments, then faded, giving the universe back its stars. Cortés had requested that the old nuclear weapon aboard his ship be armed, and then used to destroy the vessel.

"But why?" Kirk had asked. "Your people surely have some feeling for the vessel. It wouldn't hurt to leave it where it is."

"We've discussed the matter among ourselves," Cortés had told him, "and we are all in agreement that the *Hawking* should be destroyed. This is our chance for a new start, and nothing should remain of our past. We have to cut our ties with the past as a sign of commitment to our new world, as a sign that we trust the life of this planet, both human and other, and can coexist with it. Rearm the bomb, so that you don't have to waste any of your power, and destroy our ship."

Kirk had protested. "But it would be no great expense for us to use our—"

"I know," Cortés had interrupted, "I know, but it must be our choice and by our means."

"You could simply let us nudge the ship toward the sun," Kirk had said.

Cortés shook his head. "No—our way, please. I insist. We must see and know that our bomb destroys it. The reasons for this go back, go much further back than I can explain without seeming foolish. We must make this gesture as a sign of commitment and good faith, as much to ourselves as for others."

Now, as he watched the *Hawking*'s debris lose its brightness, Kirk sat back and felt tired for a moment. Another piece of history gone, he told himself, wondering how often old Earth's social disasters might have been averted if the history books had been burned, to prevent them from being misunderstood and used as a pretext for further conflict. . . .

The destruction of the *Hawking* had been Cortés's way of burning the books.

Kirk said, "Take us out of orbit, Mr. Sulu."

"Aye, aye, Captain."

McCoy leaned toward him. "Well, Jim, are you feeling a bit more hopeful about the outcome?"

"Yes, Bones, I think I am." As the *Enterprise* left orbit and swept through the space occupied only a few minutes ago by the *Hawking,* Kirk looked from McCoy to Spock and said, "Quite right, gentlemen. There's hope to spare here, and maybe a bit more."

About the Authors

Pamela Sargent and George Zebrowski have been watching *Star Trek* ever since the 1960s, when they were students at the State University of New York at Binghamton.

Pamela Sargent sold her first published story during her senior year in college and has been a writer ever since. She has won a Nebula Award, a Locus Award, and has been a finalist for the Hugo Award; her work has been translated into eleven languages. Her epic novel *Venus of Dreams* was listed as one of the one hundred best science fiction novels by *Library Journal. Earthseed,* her first novel for young adults, was chosen as a 1983 Best Book by the American Library Association. Her other acclaimed science fiction novels include *Cloned Lives, The Sudden Star, Watchstar, The Golden Space, The Alien Upstairs, The Shore of Women,* and *Venus of Shadows.* The *Washington Post Book World* has called her "one of the genre's best writers."

Sargent is also the author of *Ruler of the Sky,* a historical novel about Genghis Khan, which *Booklist* called "an impressive novel from a veteran writer," and bestselling writer Gary Jennings described as "formidably researched and exquisitely written." Her most recent novel is *Climb the Wind: A Novel of Another America,* published in 1999 by HarperPrism; Gahan Wilson called this book "a most enjoyable and entertaining new alternate history adventure which brings . . . a new dimension to the form." Among the anthologies she has edited are *Women of Wonder, The Classic Years* and *Women of Wonder, The Contemporary Years,* which *Publishers Weekly* praised as "essential reading for any serious sf fan." She is now at work on a new novel, *Child of Venus,* to be published by HarperPrism.

George Zebrowski's twenty-seven books include novels, short fiction collections, anthologies, and a book of essays. His short stories have been nominated for the Nebula Award and the Theodore Sturgeon Memorial Award. Noted science fiction writer Greg Bear calls him "one of those rare speculators who bases his dreams on science as well as inspiration," and the late Terry Carr, one of the most influential science fiction editors of recent years, described him as "an authority in the sf field."

Zebrowski has published more than seventy-five works of short fiction and nearly a hundred articles and essays, including reviews for the *Washington Post Book World* and articles on science for *Omni* magazine. One of his best-known novels is *Macrolife,* selected by *Library Journal* as one of the one hundred best novels of science fiction; Arthur C. Clarke described *Macrolife* as "a worthy successor to Olaf Stapledon's *Star Maker.* It's been years since I was so impressed. One of the few books I intend to read again." He is also the author of *The Omega Point Trilogy* and *The Sunspacers Trilogy,* and his novel *Stranger Suns* was a *New York Times* Notable Book of the Year for 1991.

With scientist/author Charles Pellegrino, Zebrowski is the author of *The Killing Star,* which the *New York Times Book Review* called "a novel of such conceptual ferocity and scientific plausibility that it amounts to a reinvention of that old Wellsian staple: Invading Monsters From Outer Space." *Booklist* commented: "Pellegrino and Zebrowski are working territory not too far removed from Arthur C. Clarke's, and anywhere Clarke is popular, this book should be, too." Zebrowski and Pellegrino also collaborated on *Dyson Sphere,* a *Star Trek: The Next Generation* novel.

Zebrowski's most recent novels are *Brute Orbits,* published in 1998 by HarperPrism, which was honored with the John W. Campbell Award for best science fiction novel of the year, and *Cave of Stars,* a new novel that is part of the Macrolife mosaic, which has just been published by HarperPrism.

Pamela Sargent and George Zebrowski are also the authors of *A Fury Scorned,* a *Star Trek: The Next Generation* novel, and *Heart of the Sun,* a *Star Trek: The Original Series* novel.

OUR FIRST SERIAL NOVEL!

Presenting, one chapter per month . . .

**The very beginning of the Starfleet
Adventure . . .**

**STAR TREK
STARFLEET: YEAR ONE**

A Novel in Twelve Parts

**by
Michael Jan Friedman**

Chapter Three

Chapter Three

President Lydia Littlejohn sat on her window sill and watched the sun melt into the mists over San Francisco Bay. She rubbed her tired eyes. Littlejohn had always believed that if Earth could win her war with the Romulans, everything after that would come easy.

As it turned out, she had been wrong.

"They should have responded by now," said Admiral Walker, a bushy-browed lion of a man in his early sixties. As usual, he was pacing the length of the president's office. "The bastards are having second thoughts."

Clarisse Dumont, a diminutive, pinch-faced woman a bit older than the admiral, shook her head. "As usual, you're jumping to conclusions. If you knew the Romulans better," she said, brushing lint off the sleeve of her woolen sweater, "you would understand they're just taking their time. They *like* to take their time."

Walker shot her an incredulous look. "*I* don't know the Romulans?" he harrumphed. "I've only been directing our forces against them for the last four and a half years."

"As I've pointed out several times before," Dumont told him with undisguised contempt, "fighting the Romulans and *knowing* the Romulans are two vastly different things."

"And how would you know that," asked the admiral, "considering you've never knocked heads with them? Never traded laser shots? Hell, you've never even seen one of their birdships."

"I've never seen a quark either," the woman countered sharply, "but I have no doubt that it exists."

Walker grunted. "You don't have to remind me about your credentials, Ms. Dumont. But a Nobel Prize in particle physics doesn't make you an expert on alien behavior."

"That's true," said Littlejohn, interceding in her colleagues' discussion for perhaps the tenth time in the last few hours. "But in addition to being one of Earth's foremost scientists, Admiral, Clarisse is also one of our foremost linguists. And without her help, we would never have gotten this far in our negotiations."

Walker's nostrils flared. "I don't dispute the value of her contribution, Madame President. I just don't see why she feels compelled to dispute the value of *mine*."

Littlejohn sighed. "We're all on edge, Ed. We haven't slept much in the last two days and we're afraid that if we say the wrong thing, these talks are going to fall apart. So if Clarisse seems a little cranky, I think we can find it in our heart to forgive her."

Dumont shot a look at her. "Cranky, Madame President? Why, I've never been cranky in my entire—"

"President Littlejohn?" said a voice.

Littlejohn recognized it as that of Stuckey, one of the communications specialists who had been coordinating their dialogue with the Romulans from an office lower in the building. The president licked her lips. "Have we received a response?" she asked hopefully.

"We have indeed," said Stuckey. "Shall I put it through, ma'am?"

"By all means," the president told him.

A moment later, her office was filled with the fluid, strangely melodious voice of a high-ranking Romulan official—not the individual actually in charge of Romulan society, but someone empowered to speak for him.

Littlejohn was able to recognize a word of the alien's speech here or there. After all, they had been negotiating the same items for days. But for the most part, it was gibberish to her.

The message went on for what seemed like a long time—longer than usual, certainly. Also, she thought, the words were expressed in an emotional context she didn't believe she had heard before. It sounded more contentious to her, more belligerent.

Oh no, the president told herself. Not another step backward. Not when it seemed as if we were getting somewhere.

Then the message was over. Dumont plunked herself down in a chair and massaged the bridge of her bony nose.

"What did they say?" the admiral demanded. "For the love of sanity, woman, don't leave us hanging here!"

Dumont looked up at him. Then she turned to Littlejohn.

"What they said," she began, "was they accept our terms. The neutral zone, the termination of their claim to the Algeron system . . . the whole ball of wax."

The president didn't believe it. "If they were going to give in across the board, why didn't they concede anything before this? Why did they seem so bloody uncooperative?"

The older woman smiled knowingly. "As I said," she explained, "the Romulans like to take their time."

Commander Bryce Shumar stood outside the turbolift doors and surveyed his base's operations center.

The place looked a lot better than it had a couple of weeks earlier. Shumar and his staff had patched up the various systems and corresponding consoles and brought them back on line. Even the weapons launchers were working again, though he didn't expect to have to use them.

Not with the war over . . .

Of course, the commander reflected, it had been easier to repair their machines than their people. He had lost eight good men and women to the Romulans, and four more of his officers might never be the same.

But they had won the war. They had beaten back the alien aggressor.

Shumar understood now where the *Nimitz* had been while his base was under attack. The ship, like half a dozen others, had quickly and secretly been moved up to the front—all so the enemy wouldn't notice that a flight wing had slipped away and made the jump into Romulan space.

The commander couldn't help applauding what that wing had accomplished. But at the same time, he resented having been left so vulnerable. He resented the deaths of the eight people who had given their lives for him.

"Sir?" said Kelly, who was again ensconced at her security console.

He glanced at her. "Yes?"

"Commander Applegate has beamed aboard and is on his way up," the security officer reported.

Shumar nodded. "Thanks."

He would have met the man in the transporter room, but Applegate insisted that they rendezvous at Ops. Apparently, the new base commander got a little queasy when he transported.

Abruptly, Shumar heard the lift beep and saw its doors slide open. A tall, fair-haired fellow in an Earth Command uniform stepped out of the compartment and nodded to him.

"Good to meet you in person," Applegate said, extending his hand.

Shumar shook it. "Same here." He indicated Ops with a gesture. "As you can see, we cleaned up the place for you."

Applegate nodded appraisingly. "If not for the burn marks," he observed, "one would never be able to tell that this facility was the focus of a pitched space battle."

Shumar winced. People who used the pronoun "one" had always bothered him. However, he wouldn't have to get along with Applegate for more than a half hour or so. That was when the *Manticore* was scheduled to leave . . . with the *former* commander of Earth Base Fourteen securely aboard.

"Well," said the new man, "I shouldn't have too much trouble here." He smiled thinly. "Running a peacetime base shouldn't be nearly as difficult as running it during wartime."

"For your sake," Shumar told him, "I hope that's true."

"Well," said Applegate, "you probably have a few things to take care of before you go. Don't let me keep you."

Shumar nodded, though he had already packed and said his good-byes. "Thanks. I'll check in with you before I take off . . . to see if you have any last-minute questions, that sort of thing."

"Outstanding," responded his successor.

The commander winced again. He didn't care much for people who used the word "outstanding" either.

Making his way to Kelly, he leaned over and pretended to check her monitors. "He's not half as bad in person as he was onscreen."

"You're lying," she replied. "I know you."

"You'll be all right," Shumar assured her.

"I won't," she insisted. She looked at him. "Promise me something."

He shrugged. "What?"

"That when you get your hands on another ship, you'll take me along."

The commander chuckled softly. "What would I do with a security officer on a research vessel?"

Kelly scowled at him. "I can do a lot more than run a security console and you know it. In fact, I was third in my high school class in biogenetics. So what do you say?"

Shumar sighed. "It doesn't pay very well."

"Neither does Earth Command, in case you haven't noticed." She glanced at Applegate. "Tell you what, I'll work for free. Just promise me."

"You would do better to hook up with Captain Cobaryn," he said. "Mapping expeditions can be a lot more exciting."

Kelly rolled her eyes. "Let's make a deal. You won't mention Captain Cobaryn and I won't mention Captain Dane."

The commander's stomach churned at the mere mention of the man's name. In his opinion, the galaxy wouldn't have lost anything if Dane had perished in the battle for the base.

"I agree," he said.

"Now promise," Kelly told him. "Say you'll take me with you first chance you get."

Shumar nodded. "All right. I promise."

"Thanks," said the security officer. "Now get out of here. Some of us still have work to do."

He smiled. "Take care, Kelly."

Patting her on the shoulder, he started for the turbolift. But he wasn't halfway there before he heard Ibañez calling him back.

"Commander?" said the communications officer.

"Yes?" responded Applegate, who had wandered in among the consoles.

Shumar looked at him and their eyes met. Then, as one, they turned to Ibañez for clarification.

"Sorry," the comm officer told Applegate. "I meant Commander Shumar."

The blond man smiled politely. "Of course." And he resumed his tour of the operations center.

Shumar made his way over to Ibañez. "What is it?" he asked.

"Commander," the man told him, "there's a subspace message from Earth. It looks like you've got new orders."

The commander felt his brow furrow. "That's not possible. My resignation was approved. After today, I'm no longer in the service."

Ibañez shrugged helplessly. "There's no mistake, sir. You're to report to the president's office."

Shumar looked at him. "The president . . . of *Earth?*"

"That's right," said the comm officer. He pointed to his

screen. "When you get there, you're to meet with someone named Clarisse Dumont. Unfortunately, this doesn't say what she wants with you."

The commander grunted. He knew Clarisse Dumont. For a short while, they had served on the same university faculty. Of course, that was before she had won the Nobel Prize for particle physics.

But what did she have to do with Earth Command? And why was she summoning him to the president's office, of all places?

"Do me a favor," Ibañez told him. "The suspense is killing me. When you get to Earth and you meet with this woman, give us a call and let us know what it's all about?"

Shumar nodded. "I'll do that," he said numbly, making another promise he wasn't sure he could keep.

Ambassador Doreen Barstowe shaded her eyes.

To the east, under a thin, ocher-colored sky that ran to a dark, mountainous horizon, a cleverly designed configuration of variously colored shrubs moved restlessly with the wind. With its twists and turns and sheer variety, it was the most impressive example of a Vulcan maze garden that the ambassador had ever seen.

Barstowe turned back to the thin, elderly Vulcan who had shown her to this part of Sammak's estate, and stood with her now on the landing behind his house. "Are you certain he's out there?" she wondered.

The attendant, who had identified himself as Sonadh, regarded the woman as if he had better things to do than escort an alien around his master's grounds.

"Sammak told me that he would be working in his garden," Sonadh assured her. "As for certainty . . . it is said that such a state can only be achieved through investigation." He lifted his wrinkled chin. "Would you like me to conduct one for you?"

Barstowe smiled at the hint of sarcasm in the suggestion. "No. Thank you anyway. I'll take a look around myself, if that's all right."

"It is indeed," the Vulcan told her. Then he turned and walked back into the embrace of his master's domicile, a sprawling, white structure whose size alone was evidence of Sammak's prominence.

The ambassador gazed out at the profusion of color again. If

Sammak was out there, she told herself, she would find him soon enough—and no doubt derive pleasure from the finding. She descended several white stone steps to the level of the ground and began her search at the only place possible—the maze's remarkably unobtrusive entrance.

The shrubs that bordered the initial passageway were a majestic golden orange, Barstowe found, lighter than the sky above them. But soon they gave way to an ethereal silver, a sprightly green, and a soft, pale yellow. It was immediately after that, in a corridor of deep, startling crimson, that she caught sight of a humanoid figure in white garb.

Sammak, she thought. No question about it. She could tell by the curling gray of his hair. The Vulcan was kneeling, pruning back a branch that had grown out too far.

He didn't turn to acknowledge his guest. Instead, he spoke a single word of recognition: "Ambassador."

Barstowe responded with the same economy. "Sammak."

Finally, he glanced at her. "I trust you are in good health."

"I am," she told him. "And you?"

"I have no complaints," the Vulcan responded.

The human touched the crimson shrubbery, which was made up of slim, pointed leaves. "I don't recall seeing this color the last time I was out here," she said. "Is it a seasonal effect?"

Sammak looked pleased. "It is," he confirmed. "In the colder months, these tuula leaves turn pink with small brown spots." He assessed them for a moment, brushing the underside of one with his forefinger. "But I have come to prefer them this way."

"So do I," Barstowe told him.

The Vulcan regarded her. "It has been a long time since last we saw each other. More than three years."

"Travel has been limited," the ambassador noted. "None of us in the diplomatic corps get around as much as we would like."

Sammak's brow creased ever so slightly. "But I do not imagine you have come to Vulcan simply to compliment me on my tuula bushes."

Barstowe smiled. "That's true. In fact, I came to give you some news. It seems the Romulans are suing for peace."

Sammak was known to be a great believer in the teachings of Surak, an individual who prided himself on his ability to master his emotions. Yet even he couldn't conceal a look of surprise . . . and approval as well, she thought.

"Peace," said the Vulcan, savoring the word.

"That's right. The Romulans were staggered by their defeat at Cheron," the ambassador explained. "If the war goes on much longer, their homeworlds will be threatened."

Sammak looked at her. "Poetic justice?"

Barstowe shrugged. "One might say that."

A few years earlier, the Romulans had pushed their offensive all the way into Earth's solar system. If not for the courage and determination of Earth's forces, the war might have ended then and there.

For a moment, the Vulcan seemed to mull over the information she had given him. "I am pleased, of course," he said at last. "As you know, Ambassador, I spoke against my world's decision to remain neutral in the conflict."

Barstowe nodded. "I recall your speech. It was quite stirring."

Sammak grunted. "For all the good it did. Clearly, neutrality was an illogical stance. If the Romulans had succeeded against Earth, they would have come after Vulcan in time as well."

"We of Earth always believed so," said the ambassador. "Together, my people and yours might have pushed the Romulans back in three years instead of five or six. And if we could have secured the aid of some of the other neutral worlds, it might only have been a matter of months."

The Vulcan sighed. "It is useless to engage in conjecture. The past is the past. Surak taught us to look to the future."

Barstowe saw her chance. She took it.

"I'm glad you hold that conviction," she told Sammak. "You see, my superiors have a revolutionary idea—one that can radically change the face of this quadrant for the better."

The Vulcan returned his attention to her, his dark eyes narrowing. "And the nature of this idea . . .?"

The human met his gaze. "I'm talking about a union of worlds," she said. "A federation designed to offer its members mutual protection against aggressor species like the Romulans . . . and maybe even facilitate an exchange of ideas into the bargain."

Sammak took some time to ponder the notion. "A federation," he repeated. He shrugged. "It is, as you say, a revolutionary concept."

"But one whose time has come," said Barstowe. "As we speak, similar conversations are taking place between Earth's ambassadors and people of vision on a dozen worlds from Sol to

Rigel—worlds like Andor, Dopterius, Arbaza, Dedderai, and Vobilin."

The Vulcan cocked an eyebrow. "I am impressed."

Barstowe smiled again. "That's a start. But what I really want—what I *need*—is your support, my friend. You see, I would like very much to present this idea to T'pau . . . and I'm sure my arguments would be more persuasive if I didn't have to present them alone."

Sammak considered the proposition for a moment. Then he nodded. "I will accompany you to T'pau's court, Ambassador. And as you suggest, we will plead your case together."

The human inclined her head. "Thank you, my friend."

Her host shook his head. "No, Ambassador. For giving me an opportunity to improve my people's lot, it is I who should thank you."

"Have it your way," Barstowe told him. "Who am I to argue with someone as eloquent as Sammak of Vulcan?"

When Admiral Walker entered the room, forty-six faces turned in his direction and forty-six hands came up to salute him.

He knew every one of them by name. Redfern, Hagedorn, McTigue, Santorini . . . Beschta, Barrios, Jones, Woo . . .

"At ease," the admiral said, advancing with echoing footfalls to the exact center of the soaring gold and black conference facility.

Earth Command's surviving captains relaxed, but not much. After all, they were men and women who had learned to thrive on discipline. That was why they were still alive when so many of their comrades were dead.

All around Walker, curved observation ports conformed to the shape of Command Base's titanium-reinforced outer hull, each one displaying bits and pieces of the visible galaxy. Only a couple of weeks ago, Earth's forces had seen the enemy abandon the last of the closer pieces.

As for those that were farther away . . . well, the admiral thought, that was the subject of this blasted meeting, now wasn't it?

"I know you've all got people you want to see and no one deserves to see them more than you do," he told the assemblage, his voice bounding from bulkhead to bulkhead. "With that in mind, I'll try to make this brief."

Forty-six pairs of eyes attended him, waiting for him to begin. Walker took a breath and did what his duty demanded of him.

"I have just come from a meeting with President Littlejohn—a very important meeting, I might add." The admiral scanned his officers' faces. "She tells me there's a change on the horizon—one that may keep us from being caught with our pants down the next time an invader comes knocking."

The prospect met with nods and grunts of approval. No surprise there, Walker mused. These were the men and women who had borne the brunt of Earth's miserable lack of readiness for five long, hard war years. No one could be happier to see some improvements made.

That is, if they were the *right* improvements.

"This change," he told them, "is manifesting itself as something called The United Federation of Planets. It's an organization that's going to include Earth and her allies. So far, we've got eight official takers. Several more are expected to follow over the course of the next few weeks."

The captains exchanged glances. They seemed impressed but also a little skeptical. The admiral didn't blame them. Nothing of this magnitude had ever been seriously contemplated.

"And that's not all," he said. "This Federation will enjoy the services of something tentatively called a 'star fleet'—an entity that draws on the resources of not just Earth, but all member worlds."

"You mean we'll be flying alongside Tellarites?" asked Stiles.

"And Dopterians?" added Beschta, obviously finding the notion a little difficult to swallow.

"Right now," Walker declared, cutting through the buzz, "the plan is for all fleet vessels to include mixed crews. In other words, we'll be working shoulder to shoulder with all Federation species."

The officers' skepticism seemed to increase. Hagedorn raised his hand and the admiral pointed to him. "Yes, Captain?"

"These fleet vessels, sir . . . where will they come from?"

"A good question," said Walker. "For the time being, we'll be pressing our Christophers into service. However, I expect we'll start building a new breed of ships before too long."

Hagedorn nodded thoughtfully. "And will our crews simply

be expanded, sir? Or will we be losing some of our human crewmen to make room for the aliens who'll be joining us?"

The admiral cleared his throat. "Actually," he told his officers with unconcealed distaste, "it hasn't been decided yet who will be asked to command these vessels."

The skepticism he had seen in his audience escalated into outright disbelief. But then, Walker himself hadn't believed it when the president apprised him of the situation.

"Sir," Beschta rumbled, "this is an outrage! We are the only ones with experience in such matters. How can an alien be expected to come out of nowhere and take command of a military vessel?"

The admiral scowled. This was the part of his presidential briefing that he had liked the least. "I truly regret having to impart this information," he told the men and women standing around him, "but there's some opposition to the idea of a purely military-style fleet . . ."

Bryce Shumar gazed at the small, wrinkled woman standing on the other side of the briefing room. "A star fleet," he repeated.

"That's right," said Clarisse Dumont. "An entity that will draw on the talents of each and every Federation member world . . . and eventually, over a period of several years, replace Earth Command and every other indigenous military organization."

"That's very interesting," the commander told her. And it was, of course—especially the notion of a united federation of worlds. "But what has it got to do with me?"

Dumont frowned, accentuating the lines in her face. "There's a lot about this star fleet that's not settled yet, Mr. Shumar . . . a lot of contention over what kind of fleet it's going to be."

The commander folded his arms across his chest, his interest piqued. "What kind of contention?"

The woman shrugged. "If people like Admiral Ed Walker have their way, the fleet will be a strictly military organization, dedicated to patrolling our part of the galaxy and defending member planets against real or perceived aggression. But to my mind, that would be a waste of an unprecedented scientific opportunity."

Her eyes lit up. "Think of it, Mr. Shumar. Think of the possibilities with regard to research and exploration. We could seek out undiscovered life-forms, unearth previously unknown civilizations. We could go where no Earthman has ever gone before."

It was unprecedented, all right. "I'm listening."

"If we're going to make that point," Dumont told him, "if we're going to establish the vision of a research fleet as something worth pursuing, we're going to need scientists in the center seats of our vessels. Scientists like you, Mr. Shumar."

He looked at her. "You're asking me to apply for a captaincy? After I spent years on a remote Earth base, watching out for Romulans and longing for the day I could return to my work?"

"I'm sure your work is important," the woman conceded. "But this is more important. This may be the most important thing you ever do."

Shumar wished he could tell her she was crazy. But he couldn't. He saw the same possibilities she did, heaven help him.

Dumont fixed him on the spit of her gaze. "Will you do it? Will you help me mold the future?"

He frowned, hating the idea of putting off his research yet again. But, really, what choice did he have?

"Yes," said Shumar. "I'll do it."

Dumont nodded. "Good. And keep in mind, you'll be receiving the support of some of the most powerful people on Earth—men and women who see this opportunity the same way we do. With even a little luck, we'll turn this star fleet into the kind of organization we can all be proud of."

Shumar figured that it was worth the sacrifice. He just wished it were someone else who had been called on to make it.

Hiro Matsura stared out a curved observation port and longed to get back among the stars.

The last two days on Command Base had been increasingly tedious for him—and he wasn't the only one who felt that way. The other Christopher captains were antsy as well. He could tell by the way they stood, the way they ate, the way they talked. They wanted out of this place.

"Touch of cabin fever?" asked a feminine voice.

Matsura turned and saw Amanda McTigue joining him at the observation port. "More than a touch," he admitted.

McTigue grunted, frowning a bit beneath her crown of plaited blond hair. "We'll be out of here before you know it," she told him. "That is, most of us. The ones they end up picking for this new fleet of theirs . . . who knows what'll happen to *them*."

"Yeah," said Matsura. "Who knows."

He knew there wasn't a chance in hell that he had been selected by the Fleet Commission. After all, he'd heard there were only six spots open, and three of them had reportedly been earmarked for non-military personnel.

Hagedorn was dead certain to get one spot, and Stiles and Beschta were the front runners for the other two. There were a couple of space jockeys deserving of the honor in Eagle and Viper squadrons as well, but Matsura's money was on his wingmates.

After all, they were the best. They had proven that over and over again. And Hagedorn, Stiles, and Beschta were the best of the best.

Suddenly, the door slid open and Admiral Walker entered the room. Matsura and McTigue everyone else in the room faced Walker and straightened, their hands at their sides. As always, Beschta thrust his rounded, stubbly chin out with an air of invincibility.

"Good morning, Admiral," said a dozen captains at once, their voices echoing in the chamber.

"Morning," Walker replied flatly, as if the word left a sour taste in his mouth. "At ease, people."

As Matsura relaxed, he noticed that the admiral didn't look happy. But then, when had Big Ed Walker *ever* looked happy?

"I've received a list of the Star Fleet Commission's selections," the admiral announced. He took in everyone present with a glance. "As I expected, three of you have been chosen to command vessels."

Here it comes, Matsura thought. He turned to Beschta, Hagedorn and Stiles, who were standing together in the front rank of the group, and prepared to congratulate them on their appointments.

Walker turned to Hagedorn. "Congratulations, Captain. You've been appointed a captain in Star Fleet."

Matsura's wing leader nodded, expressionless as always. He seemed to accept the assignment like any other.

"Sir," was his only response.

Next, the admiral turned his gaze on Stiles. "Congratulations," he remarked. "You've been selected as well."

Stiles' smile said he had only gotten what he deserved. "Thank you, sir," he told Admiral Walker.

"You're quite welcome," the admiral replied.

Beschta, Matsura thought, rooting silently for his friend and mentor. *Say the word. Beschta.*

For a moment, Walker's gaze fell on the big man and Matsura believed he had gotten his wish. Then the admiral turned away from Beschta and searched the crowd for someone else.

Damn, thought Matsura. It's not fair.

He was still thinking that when Walker's gaze fell on him—and stayed there. "Congratulations," said the admiral, staring at the young man across what seemed like an impossible distance. "You're our third and final representative. Do us proud, Captain."

Matsura felt his heart start to pound against his ribs. Had he heard Walker right? No . . . it was impossible, he told himself.

"Me, sir?" he blurted.

The admiral nodded, his blue eyes piercingly sharp beneath his bushy, white brows. "That's right, Captain Matsura. *You.*"

Matsura tried to absorb the implications of what he had just heard. "I . . . I don't . . . I mean, thank you, sir."

"Don't mention it," said the admiral.

The other captains in the room looked at one another, confused and maybe even a little angry. No doubt, they were asking themselves the same question Matsura was: why *him?* Why, out of all of the brave men and women standing in that room, had Hiro Matsura been tapped for the Federation's new fleet?

Out of the corner of his eye, he saw Beschta's reaction. The big man looked embarrassed, as if he had suddenly realized he had come to the meeting without his pants. Then he turned to Matsura.

His expression didn't change. But without warning, he brought his hands together with explosive results. The report echoed throughout the chamber. Then Beschta did it a second time. And a third.

By then, some of the other captains had joined in. With each successive clap, their number grew, encompassing the disappointed as well as the admiring. Before long, everyone but Admiral Walker was applauding, making a thunderous sound that Matsura could feel as well as hear.

The admiral nodded approvingly. Then, as the noise began to

die down, he said, "Dismissed." And with that, he turned and left the chamber.

Matsura was dazed. He couldn't bring himself to believe what had happened. However, the sadness in Beschta's eyes told him it was true.

The younger man made his way through the crowd until he stood in front of his hulking mentor. For a moment, neither of them spoke. Then Beschta shrugged his massive shoulders.

"It's no big deal," he growled. But the bitterness in his voice belied his dismissal of the matter.

Matsura shook his head. "It isn't right," he said.

Anger flared in Beschta's eyes. "It doesn't have to be right. It is what it is. Make the most of it, Hiro—or I'll be the first to tear you out of the center seat and pound you into the deck. You hear me?"

Matsura could see the pain through the big man's act. "It should have been you," he insisted.

Beschta lowered his face closer to his protege's. "Don't ever let me hear you say that again," he grated. "*Ever.*"

The younger man swallowed, afraid of what his friend might do. "Okay," he conceded. Suddenly, an idea came to him. "Why don't you sign on with me as my exec? That way, I know I'll come back in one piece."

The big man's eyes narrowed in thought for a moment. Then he waved away the idea. "I've got better things to do than be your first officer," he rumbled proudly. "There's still an Earth Command, isn't there? There are still ships that need flying?"

"Of course," Matsura assured him.

"Then that's what I'll do," said Beschta. He managed a lopsided smile. "If your fancy Star Fleet gives you a day off sometime, come look for me. I'll be the one flying circles around all the others."

Matsura grinned. "I'll do that," he answered.

But he knew as well as the big man did that Earth Command wouldn't be what it had been in the past. After all, there weren't any more Romulans for them to fight. And whenever a threat reared its head, Star Fleet would be the first wave of defense against it.

Beschta nodded his big, jowly face. "Good. And as the admiral told you . . . make us proud."

Matsura sighed. "I'll do that, too," he said.

Look for STAR TREK Fiction from Pocket Books

Star Trek: The Next Generation®

Star Trek: Deep Space Nine®

Star Trek®: Voyager™

Flashback • Diane Carey
The Black Shore • Greg Cox
Mosaic • Jeri Taylor
Pathways • Jeri Taylor

#1 *Caretaker* • L. A. Graf
#2 *The Escape* • Dean W. Smith & Kristine K. Rusch
#3 *Ragnarok* • Nathan Archer
#4 *Violations* • Susan Wright
#5 *Incident at Arbuk* • John Gregory Betancourt
#6 *The Murdered Sun* • Christie Golden
#7 *Ghost of a Chance* • Mark A. Garland & Charles G. McGraw
#8 *Cybersong* • S. N. Lewitt
#9 *Invasion #4: The Final Fury* • Daffyd ab Hugh
#10 *Bless the Beasts* • Karen Haber
#11 *The Garden* • Melissa Scott
#12 *Chrysalis* • David Niall Wilson
#13 *The Black Shore* • Greg Cox
#14 *Marooned* • Christie Golden
#15 *Echoes* • Dean W. Smith & Kristine K. Rusch
#16 *Seven of Nine* • Christie Golden
#17 *Death of a Neutron Star* • Eric Kotani
#18 *Battle Lines* • Dave Galanter & Greg Brodeur

Star Trek®: New Frontier

#1 *House of Cards* • Peter David
#2 *Into the Void* • Peter David
#3 *The Two-Front War* • Peter David
#4 *End Game* • Peter David
#5 *Martyr* • Peter David
#6 *Fire on High* • Peter David

Star Trek®: Day of Honor

Book One: *Ancient Blood* • Diane Carey
Book Two: *Armageddon Sky* • L. A. Graf
Book Three: *Her Klingon Soul* • Michael Jan Friedman
Book Four: *Treaty's Law* • Dean W. Smith & Kristine K. Rusch
The Television Episode • Michael Jan Friedman

Star Trek®: The Captain's Table

Book One: *War Dragons* • L. A. Graf
Book Two: *Dujonian's Hoard* • Michael Jan Friedman
Book Three: *The Mist* • Dean W. Smith & Kristine K. Rusch
Book Four: *Fire Ship* • Diane Carey
Book Five: *Once Burned* • Peter David
Book Six: *Where Sea Meets Sky* • Jerry Oltion

Star Trek®: The Dominion War

Book 1: *Behind Enemy Lines* • John Vornholt
Book 2: *Call to Arms . . .* • Diane Carey
Book 3: *Tunnel Through the Stars* • John Vornholt
Book 4: *. . . Sacrifice of Angels* • Diane Carey

1252.01

STAR TREK
DEEP SPACE NINE™

24" X 36" CUT AWAY POSTER.
7 COLORS WITH 2 METALLIC INKS & A GLOSS AND MATTE VARNISH. PRINTED ON ACID FREE ARCHIVAL QUALITY
65# COVER WEIGHT STOCK. INCLUDES OVER 90 TECHNICAL CALLOUTS, AND HISTORY OF THE SPACE STATION.
U.S.S. DEFIANT EXTERIOR, HEAD SHOTS OF MAIN CHARACTERS, INCREDIBLE GRAPHIC OF WORMHOLE.

STAR TREK™
U.S.S. ENTERPRISE™ NCC-1701

24" X 36" CUT AWAY POSTER.
6 COLORS WITH A SPECIAL METALLIC INK & A GLOSS AND MATTE VARNISH. PRINTED ON ACID FREE ARCHIVAL
QUALITY 100# TEXT WEIGHT STOCK. INCLUDES OVER 100 TECHNICAL CALLOUTS.
HISTORY OF THE ENTERPRISE CAPTAINS & THE HISTORY OF THE ENTERPRISE SHIPS.

ALSO AVAILABLE:
LIMITED EDITION SIGNED AND NUMBERED BY ARTISTS.
LITHOGRAPHIC PRINTS ON 80# COVER STOCK (DS9 ON 100 # STOCK) WITH OFFICIAL LICENSED CERTIFICATE OF
AUTHENTICITY. QT. AVAILABLE 2,500

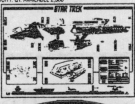

U.S.S. ENTERPRISE™ 1701 E
CUTAWAY $19.95
LTD. ED. SIGNED & #L PRINTS QT. 2,500
$40.00

AVAILABLE
NOV. 1996

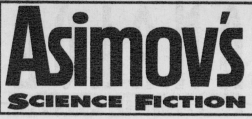